Depths

Diamondsong

A Concerto in Ten Parts

Part 09:
Depths

E.D.E. Bell

Atthis Arts
Detroit, Michigan

Diamondsong
Part 09: Depths

This is a work of fiction.
Any resemblance to actual pyrsi, winged or otherwise, is purely coincidental.

Cover Art by M.C. Krauss

Map of Ada-ji by Ulla Thynell

Interior Design by G.C. Bell

Editorial Services by:
Catherine Jones Payne, Quill Pen Editorial
Kelsey Ronan
M. Cusack

Published by Atthis Arts, LLC
Detroit, Michigan
atthisarts.com

ISBN 978-1-945009-64-8

Library of Congress Control Number: 2020940591

First Edition: Published July 2020

This book is dedicated to Camille Gooderham Campbell

for your friendship and support.

More than should have been needed!

Preface

I am often told that my writing speaks to people who have suffered repression. And I'm still learning the facets of that, in ways I could not express even recently. I now understand that my writing does largely derive from a journey of being diverted from paths I would have naturally taken, instead taking a good 43 years to be who I really am on this path that I eventually found, with a mind deeply scarred from trauma along the way. Over time, I began to see the intense pressures that were pulling me back—all the while seeing others being hurt and wanting to do more to prevent it. What I was afraid to express is that there is also great pain in connecting those two: learning that the cultures that harmed me, that I was a part of, were responsible for harming others. Thinking that I could have learned earlier. Changed earlier. These are difficult emotions to reconcile. This is a different story than that of marginalized groups. Yet, each type of harm—and the structures that foster it—are connected. I believe we need to be more open about these issues. So we can learn and improve together.

I grew up with very specific rules for how to be and not be, always lacquered with *judgment*. Also with love and joy, but the premise is still true. After 18 years, I hoped my stint in 1990s Ann Arbor would change me (I remember thinking it), but there were still too many ties (including financial) back to those pressures, complicated by what I now understand to be related and severe mental health issues, to hold me back enough that I was swept . . . into *military* culture for another 18 years. The turn of the century had very specific influences, and the currents can be strong.

None of this is easy for me to discuss, even now. Nor is this the full story. Not even close.

It took me a long time to find the words to describe who I really was, and longer to find the avenues to live it. Being vegan in a world centered on animal use as the means to connect, and regarding which your very social value is measured. Being bi in a culture that repeated, again and again, that this was abnormal and would ruin the lives of those who loved me if I ever lived it. Being an atheist in a religion-based social structure, which taught that that very structure formed the essence of good or bad—saved or damned! Being progressive: inherently compassionate in political circles that demanded fealty to what they called logic, when those same people controlled your future, your finances. Not being a man, nor relating to gender (what I've learned is called cassgender), in technical and management roles that expected both. I did my best. I tried to stand up for people. I tried.

But I didn't stand up for myself.

And that's key to standing up for *people*. If you've read this serial from a place of personal freedom, I am glad. If you've read this from a place of exploration yourself, let me offer you my best advice.

Be who you are. Don't let anyone stop you. Not the shouts, definitely not the whispers (they are worse), and not the depths.

You will get through them. And get help. Please, seek the mental health treatment you need. Even if you're not sure that you need it. Find out. Ask. Getting help will save you. You deserve it.

Yes, in this volume, another of my stories takes place underground. As you'll see through Dime's revelation, I am now committed as a writer to never doing that again, now that I understand how much of it reflects my own feelings of weight, pressure, and invisibility. That exploration has value, both to myself and readers on their own journeys, but now I have done it. Ok, one caveat—I wrote one short novel in 2018 that is, um, almost fully underground. Damn it. Yet I like the story so I will release that once I can get to editing it. But soon! To rise!

Gratitude as always to the team: Catherine Jones Payne, Kelsey Ronan, Meghan Cusack, Camille Gooderham Campbell, Sasha Kasoff Moore, Laura Johnson, Deborah Reilly, and Maria Judge. You have all done so much to lift me up. I hope you know how much.

As I recall, Volana had just flown off to call in a mysterious favor. Let's go see how that goes.

My love, E.D.E. Bell, July 2020

The World of Ada-ji

The Ja-lal: A humanoid species, dwelling in the foothills and plains of Ada-ji, characterized by broad advancements in construction, invention, and health. The Fo-ror call them brutes.

The Fo-ror: A winged humanoid species, dwelling in the forests of Ada-ji, characterized by their natural living and the use of magical powers, known as valence. The Ja-lal call them fairies.

The Ja-lal and Fo-ror are similar in form, with gray skin, but differences between them in composition and culture. Pyr is singular for a Ja-lal or Fo-ror and pyrsi is plural.

The pyrsi of Ada-ji hold many **gender identities**. While this doesn't clarify all aspects of gender, it is polite to introduce oneself with a prefix, indicating the appropriate pronouns:

- **Fe'** indicates a set of feminine identities, using the pronouns she/her/her(s).
- **Ma'** indicates a set of masculine identities, using the pronouns he/him/his.
- **Ji'** indicates a set of spectrum identities, using the pronouns ve/ver/vis.

When gender is unknown, it is polite to refer to a pyr with xe/xem/xyr(s). Any group of pyrsi (plural) would be referred to with they/them/their(s).

A pyr may be generically referred to as **Burge**, short for the more formal Burgess, often for purposes of polite address or getting a stranger's attention. This is similar to the use of Sir or Ma'am on Earth. For those who hold social prejudice based on class, the term implies some sense of status or honor.

Ja-lal and Fo-ror may live up to 50 cycles. Their lives are divided into defined **epochs**, aligning with societal expectations:

Aoch	Age 0-9	Characterized by upbringing, education, and exploration
Bakh	Age 10-19	Centered on building family, performing and completing apprenticeships, and finalizing life plans
Gamh	Age 20-29	Fully immersed in their specialty or role, contributing full-time to society
Dorh	Age 30-39	Respected in leadership and/or advisory roles; it is normal to take some time for self
Eroh	Age 40+	Expected to retire and engage in craft or occasional consulting, through the **life expectancy of around 50 cycles**.

Expectations differ for each culture. For example, while a Ja-lal must develop xyr profession into a career, a Fo-ror's profession and rank are set based on xyr social class and other historical and cultural factors.

A **cycle** on Ada-ji is perhaps up to four times the length of an Earth year. So, our main character, at age 20.5 cycles, has lived more than 80 Earth years but, in relation to her life span, could be considered at the **maturity of her early forties** on Earth.

Each **turn** on Ada-ji, a period of day and then night, is **significantly longer than an Earth day**. As such, pyrsi do not sleep according to light or dark, but instead based on their own needs, lifestyle, profession, and schedule.

The Ja-lal measure time by the periodic sounding of bells; they refer to the resultant time periods with the same term. The Fo-ror are less rigid about time-keeping and refer to the equivalent time period as a span. Each **bell**, or **span**, consists of more than two Earth hours.

Smaller amounts of time are referred to by both cultures as **takes**, which can be thought of as about ten Earth minutes.

In Earth terms, it has been about eight weeks since the beginning of our tale.

The Ja-lal and Fo-ror live on separate sides of the Great Cliff. They have not interacted since the ***Great War***, an event most noted for being the **end of the Violence** on Ada-ji.

Synopsis to Here

Just after Dime had left her career working for the Circles, the government of the Ja-lal, three hooded figures burst into her home, determined to take her away. Dime and her spouse, Dayn, ran to escape them.

The intruders were revealed to be Fo-ror, commonly called fairies. These fairies, unseen since the conclusion of the Great War, were feared and loathed by the Ja-lal, who were taught that any contact would cause the Violence to return.

Dime escaped the city and was rescued by a large animal species known as newts, where she befriended a young newt she called Juni. Dime was found there by a fe'pyr familiar with fairies, Ella, who broke the news that Dime was biologically a Fo-ror—one whose wings had been removed.

Later, Ella explained that the magical fairy power of valence did not come from the wings, but from the heart. At her recommendation, Dime traveled to the diamond caves, where she confirmed and practiced her powers. There, she discovered that the Ja-lal also have powers of valence, more internally directed. Dime believes very few Ja-lal are aware of, and thus intentionally shaping, their own powers.

Trying to make sense of these events, Dime traveled between the lands of the fairies, the Heartland, and her own Sol's Reach. She reconnected with friends: Zael, who is dying, Ador, the founder of an advocacy group called the Free Winds, Ador's spouse Batu, and Dime's own family: Dayn, Luja, and Tum. She was surprised to run into Rock, an Intel Agent and former flame, with whom she has developed a complicated friendship.

She encountered new allies: Volana, a fairy connected to a secret Fo-ror discussion group, the Foundry, Volana's friend Uchitar, who struggles with tzetz-addiction, and Hin, a young assistant Ador had taken under his charge, whose reservations about working with the fairies culminated in an incident of rudeness toward Dime.

While in the Heartland, Dime was approached by an officer of a political group, the Risers, named Intinpalo. He believes in the superiority of the Fo-ror, but an encounter with Dime's father, Gorg, may have left an impression.

Dime has met with the leaders of each land. First, High Seat Ferala, who confessed that Dime was part of an old scheme to avenge the horrors of a disease called the curse, which the Fo-ror blamed on the Ja-lal. This scheme, designed by now Third Seat Neimano, was named Project Diamondsong. His plan was to remove the wings from Fo-ror newborns, place them in positions of potential influence amongst the Ja-lal, and then allow them to grow up before activating their loyalties as Fo-ror spies. Twice, she has met with Sala, the Light, who remains resistant to her message of working with the Fo-ror.

Dime has been able to locate four other victims of Neimano: Kolk, Nafat, Olok, and Jaza, the leader of the Sol's Pillars herself.

Additionally, Dime has learned that the newts hold emotion-based valence. Stern Eyes used hers to shock Neimano, causing him to fly away, clearly injured, after he tried to attack Dime once again.

After thinking about comments Jaza had made, Dime decided she needed to find out more about Neimano's plans. She and Rock returned to the Heartland, where Tikinal, the Seats' High Clerk, directed them to meet with a secretive agent. This agent told them that Neimano was hiding a weapon: perhaps vials containing the deadly curse. Xe also suggested the newts may know the best way into the caves. When Rock and Dime traveled to ask the newts, they also learned the Circles' Boring Project had restarted, the huge drills putting both the Fo-ror and the tenuous peace at risk.

Tum is now staying with Volana's mothers, Dayn may or may not remain at the Underground, and Rock, Dime, Luja, and Uchitar are following Volana to an unknown place where she intends to call in a favor. Soon, they plan to meet Stern Eyes and Juni near a waterfall to find a passage into the caves, and hopefully destroy Neimano's weapon for good.

Ada-Ji
N
W
E
S

Depths

It was partly my own fault; but I had thought
they would understand.

—Fryderyk Franciszek Chopin, in a personal letter,
    12 September 1829

Act 1

DESCENT

Uchitar gasped as they all landed atop a rounded patio that peeked out through the forest canopy from the crown of a huge tree. As Volana trudged off toward a curtained doorway without a glance to her companions, the stunned-looking ma'pyr spun around to Dime.

"Who does she know?" he asked. Then, scanning the bench where Dime, Rock, and Luja still sat, he pulled his mouth tight.

"I know," Rock deadpanned. "It's hard to get used to seeing the style we bring to the gig."

From his twitching expression, Uchitar didn't know where to begin. Dime was pretty certain he didn't know what a *gig* was, he looked like he had thoughts about the antique, intricately carved padded seat they'd dubbed Rosebench, and there was the small matter that they'd landed unannounced at what even Dime knew had to be a very, very high-class residence. Following in the direction Volana had gone, they left the bench tucked back into the darkness. The branches rustled around them.

As any patio glowstones had either been extinguished or had faded naturally, Dime could just make out an arrangement of tables and rounded awnings that were designed to resemble tiny treetops, painted and adorned with touches of fringe. Yes, that would take a certain sort to decorate with little treetop tables while gazing out at an entire actual forest. So Uchitar had a point: whose space was this?

Dime didn't have a theory. Volana had never given indication of any secret high-class family—of course then they wouldn't be a secret. She was dating someone, Eytanii, she recalled, but Fo-ror never dated outside of their class. Not this far outside. Could this be someone Volana had cleaned for? That made the most sense. Maybe she'd cleaned a really embarrassing mess, and—

A fairy dragged xemself outside looking like xe'd fallen face first onto a board. Dime knew the feeling; the first and last time she'd entered a drinking game, waking up had not gone so well. She'd realized she didn't have the same tolerance for fermentation as others, though now she knew why. That certainly wasn't fair, she silently grumbled.

The fairy wore a large sleeping shirt of some fine, shimmery material that appeared luxurious to the touch. Xyr hair had been hastily, or so it looked, wrapped into a wide measure of dark cloth, and only a few blueish strands emerged. He sniffed a bit but didn't say anything. Dime almost laughed. There was definitely the scent of Sha-water amongst them. It had been pungent on the bench.

"This is Ma'Pyrilee," Volana said cheerfully. "He is a distinguished burgess who has joined the Foundry and he recently announced, to great cheers, that he would advance the cause of peace in any way that he could. I am so grateful he's here, roused from his slumber, providing us this opportunity to experience his greatness."

That was a lot.

The pyr's eyes had fixed directly on Rock. "Is this a Ja-lal?" he asked, punctuating both syllables. Only then did he notice Luja and Dime. He glanced at Dime's hair, then turned back to Rock. "You're all Ja-lal? Oh, wow. I imagined what you'd look like, but—" He seemed to be perking up. "I have so many questions."

Rock looked like she was holding back a retort. Dime offered her a sympathetic tilt of the head; she was sure it was a good one.

"What've you got in mind?" Rock said instead.

"How does it feel to be so smooth? With no eyebrows!"

Now Rock really looked pained. Besides, they *had* eyebrows, they just didn't let hair grow out of them.

"Burge, I'm sure you'll need to get back to your rest," Volana interrupted. "We are so grateful to you for your gifts."

"Sure," Pyrilee threw out. "Do you think we can get them to one of the meetings?" He continued to glance between Rock and Luja, who wore rather similar false grins in the darkness.

Uchitar, though handsome in the robes Volana had made him, bore patched together fabrics and a lack of adornment, and his clasped hands trembled. Dime moved closer to him.

"What do we need?" Volana continued. "We will need a place to stay and rest, out of sight and without interruption, and we will need access to food and packing material, as well as equipment such as maintenance tools and sleep supplies. Any small-group event space with lodging would suffice. Your gifts will help keep all of our loved ones safe, Burgess Pyrilee."

"No, no, it's nothing," he murmured, blinking something away. "It's thrilling to finally see all this progress. I'm honored to be at the front."

"May I write the location?" Volana sat at one of the little tables, charging a nearby glowstone just enough to write. She pulled a pencil and a scrap of inked paper from a narrow side pouch. She flipped the paper over and held up the pencil, looking expectantly at Pyrilee.

"Sure, that's fine. I won't be using it for a bit anyway." Pyrilee rubbed the side of his face as he listed what sounded like a Pito address. Dime was used to streets and towers but here locations seemed to be more numerically based.

Dime thought she heard a voice from inside. Not a happy voice. "That should work." Pyrilee added, "I can have anything delivered that you want."

"No, Burgess, we should have what we need there." Volana

handed him the paper, presumably so he could check her notes. "Your support is marvelous. May Sha's gifts return to you."

"That's it." Scribbling a quick initial, he handed it back, then glanced toward the curtain. "Anything you find there is yours," he said with a distracted nod. "I must insist."

Having a sudden idea, Dime scrambled in her bag, pulling out a paper and pen. To her amusement, she realized it was Ferala's gold engraved pen. She covered it with her fingers, but then decided a gold pen probably wouldn't catch the pyr's notice. Hastily, she wrote who Tum was with, said she had to take another journey and had Luja with her, said to tell Dayn she missed him, corner-folded the note, and wrote Ador's name across the front. She put the pen back in her bag.

"Burge Pyrilee," she said. "Are you able to have this flown to the Crossing and sent to the pyr Ador of Lodon? They will know him." She knew she was supposed to offer something in return, but he'd said he'd make deliveries, so hopefully this didn't go too far.

She didn't expect him to grin. "A resistance letter. My first. I'll have it delivered right away."

"Thank you," Dime said, bowing a bit.

He'd already turned, to Luja this time. His words were rushed. "What are the towers like? Are they as tall as they say?"

Luja hesitated. "Yes. And some are smaller. Maybe with your help this night, we'll live in a world where you can visit." Ve glanced to Dime.

Pyrilee's unpadded shoulders rose, his sleepwear shimmering. He turned back to Rock, a question on his lips. A few birds chirped from the sides, and he paused.

Volana stepped forward. "Perhaps I will see you at the next meeting?"

"I can be there," he said, relaxing back again. "Drop the schedule with my servants."

"We will," Volana said. She seemed to be considering how to say something. "If we all continue to let others know of these efforts, we can bring other important voices into the dialogue." She paused. "The change will not be easy."

Pyrilee's eyelids were drooping. "Ok, great." His fingers twitched against his side.

The voice called again through the curtain, and without a goodbye, Pyrilee disappeared.

"Is he . . . coming back?" Rock asked, sounding as amused as she was curious.

"Let's go," Volana said. "I was trying to figure how to not have him witness your flight anyway. I'll check back with him soon. Let's go to where he's sent us. Better to arrive before the light."

For a stride, Dime thought she was talking about Sala, but then realized she meant Sol's rise. She was immensely curious where they'd be going, and how it would compare to this. Of course, they hadn't even gone inside; this was just his patio. His bedroom patio? Who knew.

The destination turned out not to be far away. Though solidly in the city, it was secluded in a dense section of forest. Unlike his residence, which had been surrounded by such thick brush that Dime couldn't tell how large it was beyond the treetop patio, this structure was visible from approach, as if cleared for the nearly 360 view. Three full stories were firmly nestled against one wide, old tree, not close to the ground, but not so high up either. Clustered pipes ran up the tree's trunk and out of sight. A woodplank deck surrounded the entire upper level. They landed Rosebench there, next to a large curtain, and walked through. Dime set her bag near the entrance, as Uchitar and Volana slipped on their tree shoes.

Dime still had some in her bag, but since Lu and Rock didn't and the floor wasn't carpeted, she just kept with her boots. No one was even here. Or at least, she hoped.

"Hello?" Volana called. "Is anyone here? Hello?" With clear relief at the lack of response, she charged a few of the glowstones, setting the space into soft light.

What Dime saw next could only be described as . . . a party room.

Not that Dime had spent a lot of time at parties and certainly not party rooms. But she'd worked for the Circles long enough to see and recognize one.

The spacious lounge, surrounded by draped windows, had no interior walls or other barriers except a few winding countertops, allowing partial privacy in some of the seating. Only three sections felt separate: one a bar area, that looked to have running water and a large counter, likely with storage. The second had a curtain tied back to reveal a long hallway, which Dime assumed to lead to washrooms affixed to a different part of the tree. Only this area was lacking windows, as it must be facing the tree's trunk. And on the side furthest from the entrance, the floor appeared to drop off behind a railing; Dime figured this was a staircase to the two lower levels.

Volana flapped over to a table, inspecting the surface. She twisted around to survey the room, keeping one hand over her midsection.

"Very recently cleaned. By pyrsi who don't much like him."

"How can you tell that?" Luja asked, stepping over. "You can tell emotions? From cleaning?"

"Most certainly you can. Look here—the surfaces are impeccably cleaned. You probably don't want to know the weight of bottles they flew back, either. Everything taken care of, all the tick marks ticked. That's because they like having high class connections and there are many worse roles out there. But—" She raised a finger. "The undersides of the table are sticky. The floor is surface-swept only. Look at the trim." She shook her head despite Dime having no idea what trim she was talking about. They'd been there only a few strides. "Things he wouldn't notice. Just enough to do the job."

Dime walked around, taking in the décor—a strange mix of simple and showy, one that wouldn't be seen in Lodon. While geometric and elegant curves flowed through unpainted beams and wood insets to the glossy floor, each step revealed an unexpected accent: an inlaid table, a carved handrail, a wall sculpture. Sure, the Circles' complex had pillars and ledges with such detail, but the complex made no secret that it was there to impress. Neither did this place, but it was somehow showier, in the way that luxury was woven through each simple board. Like it didn't need to be there, but it was.

As huge as this upper level was, she was curious about the two below. Well, they had permission to be here. The pyr had given them an indefinite stay with no spoken restriction. While she wasn't trying to take advantage, the space seemed of little import to him. Luja, likely thinking along the same lines, joined her as she walked back to an elegant banister, that crept up from what turned out to be a curved ramp.

Unlike a staircase with a narrow entry, here there was a rather wide swath cut into the floor. Luja peered down. "You could just fly down if you wanted. Or, you know, flap?"

Dime, used to stairs, found herself using the railing as they awkwardly walked down the slanted floor. As it eventually leveled out, she saw a small, teardrop-shaped room, clearly there to block the rest of the floor from view. Plush rugs, gilded statues, and strands of crystals graced the small lobby, if that was the right term. Without chairs or tables or any functioning equipment, it didn't appear there was anything to do here other than continue downstairs or walk through the single curtain, hanging inconspicuously to the side of a huge mirror.

As they passed through the curtain, a hallway bent around, opening after two curves into a long central corridor between large, open rooms. One side was dedicated to storage; tall shelves of longer-term food supplies stood alongside empty bins where fresh items could be placed. A few such items waited: fruits, wrapped cremas, and even loaves of bread, picked through as if there'd been an event here recently. Aisles of racks held decorations for any type of occasion, and also specialized items like musical instruments and dance accessories such as ribbons and bells. She did resolve to look at the instruments more, later.

The other side opened to a large kitchen and workshop area.

The space was as plain as could be, but despite the lack of aesthetics, it was the finest kitchen she'd ever seen. Huge metal surfaces straddled a series of clay stoves. All types of small chopping devices, wood boards, pots, and pans lined the walls. Bowls and utensils hung from custom hooks, alongside oddly shaped, unfamiliar items.

Luja had picked up a thin, ribbed board.

"Pasta," Dime said, remembering where she'd seen something similar made of pottery, in Lodon. "You roll pasta against it and it gives the sides a pattern. Just little chunks." She demonstrated with imaginary pieces of dough, wondering what grain they used here for pasta, without any plains to grow it. The bread she'd had at Volana's and during her prison meal had been delicious, though with a different taste than she was used to.

"Does it taste better with ridges in it?" Luja was turning the pasta board in vis hands.

"Yeah. It sort of does. It's texture," she explained. "And it holds the sauce."

Ve eyed the board as ve set it down.

Moving to the lowest floor, there was a larger version of the fancy lobby, but this one was bordered by a series of eight curtained doorways, each on its own section of wall. Stepping through the closest, they found a complete home, except for kitchen and utility areas. A large bed, an individual washroom, and a cozy seating nook facing a wide window—that in the daylight would frame a breezy world of green—completed the suite.

"This is his extra place," Luja noted.

Dime could only think of that bed. It looked like a *nice* bed. They trudged back up the ramp, to find Volana still standing near the entrance tapping her hands together and Rock and Uchitar leaned against a table sharing a pitcher of water.

"We need to get some rest," Rock said, seeing Dime. "I know finding this . . . thing . . . is important but we've been up for a lot of bells now." Though they'd only had one good sleep at Batu's, Dime also remembered Rock had been stuck in that room with

Jaza. The thought made her sick, but she forced herself to focus. Rock couldn't have been sleeping well. She was right. They needed to rest.

Oh. "Can we move Rosebench in?" Those cushions could get funky if it rained.

"Aww, you're fond of it! I picked it," Rock bragged to Luja.

"Never mind," Dime said. "I keep forgetting. I can move it." She walked out, and using valence, guided the padded bench into the room, positioning it against one of the sides. Actually, it looked great in here, under a glossy red wall sculpture. Maybe they would give the party fairies some ideas.

She stifled a yawn. "There's rooms on the lowest floor. Plenty of space for everyone." She stopped. "Not even rooms. Whole suites."

"With their own showers," Luja added, holding vis arms.

"Anyway, rest first, figure it out later?" Everyone nodded. "Volana," Dime started through a huge yawn that had finally escaped, "are you staying here or going home?"

"I'll stay here," she answered. "I'm sure the bed is better than mine, and then I'll be around if there's an issue. I did ask him to keep pyrsi away, and I think he'll honor that. But you never know what else could happen." Now she yawned, and with Uchitar offering her an arm, they walked down the ramp together. Luja looked away, and Dime realized ve'd been hoping to see how the fairies flew down it. But Volana and Uchitar were both not in their strongest state. The ramp was probably a relief.

"Raid the bar?" Rock grinned.

Dime turned in disbelief.

"Look, I have issues. And I'm not saying we have a lot—we have to get to bed, and I am eager to use one of those fancy, private showers to rid the Sha-itch from my skin. The gust of wind helped, but it didn't get *everywhere.*"

Luja grinned at that, now moving vis arms as if resisting the urge to sluff off whatever was still under vis sleeves. "I know. I mostly followed Ma-ma to make sure there were showers here."

"Or what?" Dime said with a laugh. "Volana finds us a richer friend?"

Luja cocked vis head. "The itch is serious."

Rock pointed at Luja in agreement as she walked over to the bar. "Just figure this guy has the good stuff and would never miss it." Ducking down for a stride, she popped back up, holding a small cobalt blue bottle and wriggling out a black stopper, centered with a glittering crystal. "Is this real?" She held the stopper in her hand, as the glowstones from the other side of the room passed through and laid faint rainbows across the back wall.

Dime knew she meant the diamond in the stopper, which was indeed a diamond. But she didn't need to answer that. Rock had used valence herself, and certainly knew the effect of the unique crystals. By Luja's stare, ve knew as well.

"He uses it to store ferm," she said, at a loss of what else to add.

"Everything you find there is yours," Luja repeated, pulling out three pink cut-glass—Dime hoped these at least were cut glass—fingerwells from a cabinet, appropriately sized to the petite bottle.

"I give up," Dime said, trying not to notice Rock pouring her child a shot of whatever was inside. At least Rock's pour to the Aoch was a bit smaller.

Expecting some throaty burn, Dime was surprised to find that the liquid was clean, like the purest water with a hint of flower blossom essence. As she set the glass down, a strange sensation moved up into her nose.

"Was this a bad call?" Luja sounded nervous and had rested a hand on the side of vis own nose. "I've never heard of this."

Dime considered with unease that Luja, a medic trained in mind-altering substances, did not know what was happening.

"No way," Rock whispered, staring across the room.

"Are you having visions?" If their demise was nigh, Dime at least wanted to hear about the visions.

"No! But I think this is fairyblood."

Dime straightened.

"No! Sorry! It's what solies call it. It's not blood-related. *Obviously.*" Rock glared at her. "I heard about this stuff. Not sure what fairies call it, but it's super pricey at the Crossing. They say it makes your vision sparkle. Honestly, I doubted it was real."

"What?" Luja stared down at the glass. "What does that *mean*?"

Dime wondered if ve'd had ferm before, but didn't really want to ask. If not, this was shaping up to be a unique first experience. Dime gasped. The room, only lit by a few of the glowstones, sparkled in little dots, as if tiny crystals in the air reflected a source of unseen light.

"Whoa," Luja whispered.

And no one argued when Rock reached down for a large, plainish bottle, and poured three shots of a dark liquid into three lowballs. She slid each across the lacquered wood bar, down the blue resin river running through it. Dime looked at the new glass: it wasn't too fancy, just some etching. She knocked the drink back, a familiar burn on her tongue.

"Time for bed?"

"Time for shower. Then bed."

Dime felt an unusual sense of elation and couldn't be annoyed when the other two started giggling. Slowly, they made their way down the now-glittering ramp and each selected one of the remaining suites, glad to see the fairies had marked their own by moving the little side tables in front, each holding a thin vase with dried sprigs. Dime wondered if this was fairy custom or just her friends being innovative.

Making her way inside and dropping outer clothes on a path to the washroom, she could already hear the rush of water through the walls, continuing as she tucked into the soft bed.

The sparkling did not stop when she closed her eyes, yet she felt unusually at ease, falling fast asleep.

Plates of fresh sliced toma fruit had been set out on the third-floor tables, each piece sprinkled with salt and pepper and served with a little whipped crema—boughfruit, she guessed. Uchitar was walking around with a pot, ladling out a soft grain mixture to the side.

"Thank you, Uchitar," they said in turn, and Dime was glad to see him smiling. He moved slowly, but otherwise looked well enough to accompany them.

Sol had risen, probably long ago, but they kept the curtains drawn, and so the glowstones were still providing most of the light to the large upper level. Scanning the room in all its opulence, Dime couldn't help but think of Volana's humble dwelling in a slightly creaky tree. She'd rather be there.

Though, the private indoor shower had been nice.

Soon they'd be off. Dime didn't want to keep the newts waiting at the meeting point; it was probable they were already there. "Volana, Juni and Stern Eyes seemed a little uncomfortable about the meeting place." She took out her notes as well as the map Volana had previously drawn, and she smoothed the papers over the table. "From what we gathered, it's around here." She pointed. "I guess it's a sizable waterfall?"

"You are meeting . . . newts there?" Volana drew her mouth in. Uchitar, pot in hand, leaned in over the table. His wings twitched.

Dime never liked not knowing what pyrsi's faces were about. Or wing twitches, now that that was a thing. "Yes, that's the place? Is it a mystical site or something? Guarded by a giant beast?"

Uchitar went to take the pot back downstairs, and Volana stepped back, straightening. "No," she said. "It's a gorgeous neigh-borhood. It's just very popular. All high-class burgesses, hard to get into, and unlike here"—she swung her arms around—"very dense. To fit everyone in. And you want to fly through it with newts." She caught herself. "Walk through it, I mean."

"That's the plan, unless you have a better one."

Rock had already started cutting the toma slices with the side of her fork. Cutting, loosely, more like wiggling. Luja still wasn't up.

"You know," Volana finally conceded, "I have enough going on. You want to walk through Pito with newts, you walk through it with newts." She flung a hand like she couldn't believe what she was saying.

"Alright, so that's a plan." Dime's reality had slipped long ago. "Anyway," she said, folding the papers and setting them on another table for now, "they're the ones who know where the passage is, so we'll show up, let them smell us, and then follow them into the ground."

There was no response to that except chewing sounds. Dime decided she needed some brew. After getting down to the kitchen and finding a nice dark roast with a deep, rooty smell, she was glad to see that Uchitar was enjoying his meal and Luja had joined everyone.

"Pleasant wake, Lu."

"Pleasant wake, Ma-ma."

Dime almost suggested a nap after Uchitar's lovely biscuit, but now she knew she was just stalling. That bed had been so comfortable, she felt like she'd slept three times. "Supplies?" They walked down the ramp, Dime going slowly again so she wouldn't trip on the incline.

Food and wrappings were easy enough; the kitchen was stocked with about anything they'd think to take, at least the fairy interpretation of it. As for comfort, Dime and Rock already had thin travel blankets in their bags, but they decided strapping on a fluffy pillow couldn't hurt. Uchitar and Luja found their own sleeping materials, each to taste, and Luja picked up extra rope to tie items to vis bag. Ve was starting to look like a festival pole, Dime thought.

Ve'd also found a sealed roll of ground dein, and muttering that they might not have another hot meal for a while, had started frying up some patties.

"We just ate," Dime said.

"It's a snack," Luja retorted. "For the road."

Dime wasn't sure about this until she heard the patties sizzling over a stove. And she didn't argue when Luja handed two of them over, wrapped with some dal crackers in a large crispleaf. Rock had suddenly appeared behind her, and Dime snuck past, finishing the warm wrap as she went back to checking their supplies.

She noticed that Volana was hovering a bit, as if to catch her alone. Taking the hint, Dime stepped into the pantry area. She was glad that Volana followed. Had this been a Lodon room, she could have closed the door for privacy, but here there was only another curtain, pulled open over a broad hook. Of course, closing either a door or a curtain would draw attention.

Volana kept her voice low. "Uchitar is working very hard for you to not see his symptoms," she said. "Keeping him distracted will be good for him, but he must eat, must rest, must have water, and must not be left alone."

"Does he . . . have any tzetz?" Dime didn't know how else to ask but directly. She looked up at the fairy.

Volana started fiddling with one of the ribbons on her robes. "He says he doesn't and I believe him."

That was a harsh thing to add. Rock had been so sure, before, that Uchitar wouldn't break a promise to Volana. But lying, that would be another level.

"It is his mind that is the most concern. This is part of my thinking. He isn't well-suited to the Foundry work. He's a builder. Sitting around bores him. And I just can't watch him all the time." Her face twisted. "I'm tired. I try to help—"

Dime sighed. Volana had seemed more chipper in the Underground, but she'd been, for once, not taking on the constant care of others. And just afterward, Uchitar had relapsed. She wondered if Volana felt guilty, but suggesting she should not could also raise the thought, if she didn't have it. "I think I understand," Dime tried. "You've been the very best friend he could have. Let me be a friend now, too."

"Eytanii hasn't returned my notes," she added, out of nowhere, letting go of the ribbon.

Dime was hesitant to intervene; she hadn't even met the pyr. "If you need time to connect back with him, I think we're all set here."

She tried to give the fairy her warmest smile, though she often fell short in moments like this.

"We should go to the others," Volana said.

Her heart sank for the younger pyr's worry. She knew Volana had been dreaming of parenting her ba'pyr together with Eytanii. And Dime couldn't help but read into her affect now. Yet, anytime she'd given a pyr relationship advice, even so much as 'trust yourself', it seemed the pyr had gone the other way. This had made for a few awkward biscuits with reunited couples. So Dime never knew what to say.

"Our roads can lead strange places," she offered, not really knowing why she'd said something so ethereal and not helpful. She wasn't even sure Volana heard; the fairy had returned to the larger room. When Dime joined her, she was already showing Luja how a collapsible cooking pot worked as Luja set the pan ve'd used out to dry. The smell of hot oil and spices hung in the air, though it didn't make her hungry, as full as she was.

Dime sat back onto the floor, mentally inventorying what she'd packed and what she still might want. There was only so much room.

When they were ready to go, Volana seemed distant. Yet when Dime offered her the bridge, Volana took it for a hug and pulled her in. "This is as close as I get these days," she said.

That was as close as Dime's friend-hugs got all the days, but she decided not to get into that.

Truly, Dime had no idea how much longer Volana had in her pregnancy. She hadn't been pregnant herself—she'd learned when this first started she could not have been, because her biology was fairy and Dayn's soly. Her family growing up had just been Gorg and herself. She'd had some pregnant coworkers, but each body changed differently.

So she wasn't sure how close Volana was. But the fe'pyr was looking increasingly tired. That said, perhaps they all were.

Dime released the fairy and was glad to see her smile. In that moment, she had a thought. Since this ordeal started, all the things that had been difficult had circled in her mind, and trying to relax sometimes felt like juggling them, tossing each away knowing it would return. Learning about her past. Losing her home. Moving her family from place to place and knowing they'd seen the Violence, seen its threat.

But there was joy, too. Always joy. Would she ever have met the fairies that she now considered friends? Strong Volana. Pyrsonable Uchitar. Elegant Tikinal. While at first, their wings and hair stood out to her as signs of a different life, she didn't notice those commonalities as such now. She saw beautiful, individual pyrsi. With their own culture. But also the same.

"Do you need anything?" Volana's face held concern.

Well, look, she couldn't always prevent a bit of musing.

It was who she was.

"I'm fine," she answered, shaking herself back to the present. "Just thinking how grateful I am, for all of you."

"I feel the same," Volana said. "Now, are you all ready to go?"

There was a solemnity to the procession as Dime lifted Rosebench back outside. With heavy eyes, Volana bid the group farewell and flew off, her robes fluttering under her wings as she disappeared into the trees.

"Can I help?" Dime asked Uchitar, who slumped back against the wall, his elbows propped against a window ledge. "Get you anything?"

"Let's go," he said. "I'll be fine."

Together, one bench and one fairy, they flew off toward the sur side of Pito, Dime concentrating to keep them from view, always a challenge in the densely populated forest, but even more so on a colorfully-upholstered bench.

Rock held the map; she seemed to concentrate just as hard as she looked for landmarks and remembered Volana's pointers. And then, hearing the roar of the waterfall in the distance, Dime finally grasped what Volana had been saying.

The river swelled into a lake, bordered by tall trees. A sheet of rock stood high on the nor end, water cascading over it and plunging into a wild spray before the white froth gave way to a deep blue, joining with varied strands of verdure and lighter tones of sky as it calmed and narrowed back into the flowing river.

The trees reverberated with structures and life: a few distant squeals of ch'pyrsi and the rumble of conversation. Pyrsi lounged on decks, spread out in the stripes of Sol, and purple-winged fairies fluttered around and across, as light reflected like giant glitter on the ripples of the lake below. The air smelled of trees and water and Sol, all at once. She wished Tum and Dayn could see this, as Luja gazed, wide-eyed, at all of it.

So much to take in. Sparkle and colors and wings and laughter. The simplicity of pure beauty with luxury layered in. A little like the Grand Resort of Nor Lodon, there wasn't a space without celebration and life. Except, here, that included the skies as well, as pyrsi traveled between the water and the dense neighborhood within the trees.

How was she going to fly a couch into this?

"What about compost?" Rock asked. "You seem to do well with that."

"A place like this?" Uchitar answered while Dime was absorbing the comment. "Fliers move it well away from here. These kind of homes don't even have chutes." He was growing out of breath and Dime realized, unlike her use of valence to keep the bench in the air, Uchitar was flapping his wings in place. They needed to land.

"What if I distract them?" he asked.

Dime glanced over. What, he'd distract the whole lake? They didn't need the whole lake, she supposed.

Uchitar pulled back a one-sided grimace. "Look, down there, that low patio."

Dime would have called it a high patio, but then again that was from the perspective of the ground or a single floor level. Compared to the layers of life throughout the trees, that patio was low indeed.

"It's designed to let pyrsi watch the river. So what if I keep them watching the river, while you land under it?"

Dime wasn't even going to ask. She nodded.

Uchitar flew out over the water, in front of where pyrsi were enjoying what looked like tall glasses of a gold juice. Or ferm? Probably both.

Flapping his wings vigorously, he began to bellow out in a surprising bass tone. Some sort of folk song, she figured.

She couldn't make out the words from where she was, but Uchitar clapped with the rhythm and sang with percussive force.

As the pyrsi all turned to stare, Dime took the chance and dove the couch underneath the wide patio. Seeing, as she neared, that not every pyr had craned to see what the singing fairy was doing, Dime brought the water of the river up into a quick frothy spray, shielding them as they rushed between the tall beams holding up the structure. Thinking quickly, she whisked the spray upward, sending it toward Uchitar, as if he'd made the elaborate staging for himself, indulging in a bit of artistic valence.

Leaving the bench, she picked through the brushy grass they'd swept through and walked out to one of the front beams. A voice cried out from above. "Get out of here! Your fun's over!" She hoped they were calling to Uchitar only. She hoped he had a plan to get out.

"Any more and we'll call a marshal!"

"Back to the canals, friend!"

Harm. Dime hoped there wasn't a marshal watching already.

"Please! Don't call a marshal!" Uchitar replied. "It was a dare!"

She supposed that meant he dared himself.

To a few jeers and chuckles but mostly the return of talking and clanking, Uchitar flew off, winding through the trees and out of sight.

Dime turned to see Luja and Rock already next to her. Rock was holding Dime's bag, which she took.

Rock sneezed. "Oh, Sol, let's get out of here fast. Something is in my nose down here."

Dime glanced back. Even from this short distance, she could no longer see Rosebench, either through the patio's deep shadows or the rustling brush. Hopefully ve'd be fine. "Let's move this way," Dime said. She almost said that they needed to meet up with Uchitar, Stern Eyes, and Juni, but Rock knew that.

They edged over, watching the banks and the sky to make sure no one was in view. Dime squinted in the bright light, the upstream waterfall reflecting it in dazzling bursts. It had been such a long, intense night, and then the borrowed home had been kept dark, or at least they hadn't let Sol's light into it for fear of being seen. So she took in the warm light, just a stride, knowing she'd soon be away from it again.

That thought had her sinking, even as she grasped at the joy of the sensation. She loved the nighttime, but pyrsi weren't built to be away from the light for too long. Yet they couldn't stay here. She glanced around, hoping the newts had found somewhere they could hide. Being spotted even once would cause an uproar of hundreds of pyrsi. Dime didn't even want to think about it.

Juni almost knocked her over. *Sol!* She hadn't heard the newt coming. Stern Eyes was right behind her. Juni sniffed back at the wispy brush.

"See," Rock said. She and Juni exchanged a look.

It wasn't until then that Dime realized the flaw in the plan. How were they going to talk to their friends without Tum to translate? "Lu?" she asked in a whisper.

"Yes?"

"Can you talk to them?"

Luja grinned. Apparently ve *had* thought about this. "Not like Tum-Tum. But I can get by." Ve greeted Juni and Stern Eyes, who murmured back. Still, Juni edged over, running her hands down Dime's side in a way that was almost polite.

"Can you tell them we're waiting on Uchitar?" The newts wouldn't know he'd been added to the party.

Ve clicked awkwardly, stumbling over sounds and gestures. Juni responded with a motion of her hand, firm like a proclamation. Stern Eyes looked unsure. She supposed they should have asked the newts before adding a fairy, but then, they saw Dime as a fairy. She wished everyone could just accept each other. It was the pyrsi at fault for those divisions, she reminded herself. Not the newts. Luja repeated Juni's gesture.

"What's that?" Dime peered over at Lu's extended hand.

"Just like we don't know their names, they actually think we don't have names at all. We haven't earned them. So, we compromised on these gestures for each of us. This one," ve punctuated the motion, "is now Uchitar."

"What does that mean?" It wasn't anything obvious, like a hammer or wings.

"Who knows. None of them seem specific."

"Well I hope non-specific hand gesture fairy gets here soon," she said, mostly to herself. Rock sneezed again. "I hope he's ok." The sudden idea that maybe Uchitar had been led off by a marshal had wrested her heart. She was already thinking through the complicated dynamics of a second prison rescue, and how she'd promised to announce herself but Tikinal had said not to go—when Uchitar landed to their side. His flapping wings disturbed the brush, sending Rock into a sneezing fit.

"Anyone following?" Rock choked out.

"I don't think so," he said. "Hello," he said to the newts, looking totally unconcerned at their presence. They both grunted.

"That was great," Rock added, "but we'll talk about it later." She sneezed again.

"So the question is—" Dime started.

"Do we need a lot of questions now?" Rock had a finger under her nose and her head was bobbing, as if she were trying to control any impending sneezes.

"Sorry, just one. One of the newts will lead, but do we creep slowly, or do we book it?"

"Let's ask them," Luja said.

Rock nodded at ver, then buried her nose into the top of her shirt.

Slowly, Luja struggled to make the newt sounds. Stern Eyes coached ver, like a cub, and Dime had the impression Luja was repeating verself. Maybe this was going to be challenging after all.

"I think," ve said, "they are saying once we go, we have to keep going. They said the tunnel entrance is close to the waterfall. We have to go on that path." Luja pointed out at the tumbling water, surrounded by the sizable lake. Where ve pointed, the side of the rockface was covered with the spray that drifted to the side of the falls. Leading that way was a wide patch of open shore, stretching away from the line of trees, and without fairy structures since it was so directly in the path of the mist. And probably very loud. Dime couldn't see what path the newts meant, but it was clear they had to get closer to the falls to find it.

Fast or slow, they couldn't risk the newts being seen. They probably made it here ok because they crept through shadows and under the structures. She pictured Juni out on that empty shore in the sunlight. Everyone would spot her. And it's not like they wouldn't draw attention walking in a big blanket or something—an idea she never would have even had during her life in Lodon, she considered. The Circles banning head coverings used to feel logical; now it felt as the Violence. Who was any pyr to force another to show or conceal xyr skin? *Oh!*

Dime remembered how Stern Eyes had run away after the attack, what she thought she'd seen there. "Ask if they can conceal themselves . . . with their valence."

Uchitar didn't know about the newt valence, to her knowledge, but she was glad he held his countenance, only flinching a little.

Anyone willing to undertake this dangerous journey simply needed to be trusted. And that was it.

It was clear that neither newt had fully grasped what Dime had said. As Luja stumbled through it, Stern Eyes stifled a cry. Juni rolled into a ball, covering her head with her arms. At least she wasn't digging a hole to hide in; Rock wouldn't appreciate any further disruption of the brush. Seeing her friend still breathing through her shirt, Dime tried to signal her an apology, but Rock gestured her on.

"We have to hurry. Luja, just say we won't tell, and we don't want them to be seen."

Stern Eyes tapped her hands onto the ground dismissively. As if the decision was made, her eyes set—more than normal—and she faded into almost a thin film or shadow. From the shimmer, she grunted something, and grunting back, Juni disappeared in a similar way.

Luja stepped forward with a branch covered in dead leaves, and soon it waved forward like a floating flag, as ve lowered vis hand.

"I gave that to Juni," ve clarified. "I think. And asked them to lead. I don't know which one is leading and I hope I didn't disturb some power dynamic with the branch. Either way, there they go," ve suddenly added.

"Thank the Light," Rock added through her shirt, with a wink to Dime, as they started to follow.

"Uchitar, can you keep your wings sort of prominent?" Harm, that sounded weird. Hopefully he'd know what she meant. Just while they were so close to other pyrsi. Anyone peering down would hopefully just see his wings. And hopefully not recognize him.

"Good idea," he answered, dropping back behind them and flapping his wings as they moved to catch up with the floating tree branch.

Luja kept giggling.

"What?" Dime whispered.

"I'm sorry," ve said. "I know it was my idea but what if someone saw that branch? Is that better?"

"Actually it is," Uchitar said. "They'd think we're just messing around with valence."

"Oh." Luja paused. "See, I'm smarter than I know."

"We usually are," Rock said.

"Is it the same," Dime asked, "how they disappear? From what you showed me before?" Tum had been experimenting with causing her skin to take on impossible colors, something Dime actually tried not to think about too often.

"I'm not sure," Luja answered. "It's different, but I don't know how much the same it is too. When we change our skin, we are making a change inside our bodies, pulling from a place I don't understand. They are not changing. They are still fully there. But they use emotion, I believe something like our frustration, to stop us from fully seeing them.

Sometimes frustration made Dime feel invisible too. Yet, it was hard to get used to the literal manifestation, the branch with its dried leaves bobbing happily in the air, like Juni might actually be enjoying the excursion. Perhaps that was an illusion as well.

She kept an alert eye as they moved steadily along the shoreside brush and toward the waterfall, toward where they'd expose the group to a broader view. Not seeing anyone around but knowing anyone could see them from a distance—and hopefully figure they were a group of wandering fairies—she decided talking was not a concern.

"Uchitar, may I ask what that song was? Unless it's pyrsonal, of course."

She didn't expect him to laugh.

"Sorry, it's just like the *least* pyrsonal song. It's called 'Boots in the River' and it's a game that ch'pyrsi play."

A few steps later, he swung around. "I still can't get over it," he added.

"Over it?" Dime didn't know what he meant.

"Since the first flap I met you, I knew I was seeing someone different. Yet, look, I'm here around a whole group of solies." Volana must have taught him the term. "And we're so similar in so many ways." He stumbled over a rough patch of ground but before Dime could worry too much, he was continuing. "We're so similar. Yet none of you have heard of something so universal as 'Boots in the River'."

I guess universal depends on your universe, Dime thought. "You'll have to teach us to play it sometime."

Uchitar didn't respond, and his wings were still flapping with strength. She thought back to what Volana had said, about Uchitar hiding his symptoms. He'd acted so energetic, she kept forgetting. She hoped she hadn't asked too much of him. "You know, you don't have to hold your wings up anymore. I think we're far enough away now." In fact, she could see the shore glistening up ahead, wet from the waterfall's mist. A host of brightly-colored flowers grew there, thriving in conditions Dime could never have imagined in Lodon.

"I'm fine," Uchitar said.

The bobbing branch stopped at the water's edge, and the others with it. Dime's concern grew when she saw, closer now, the path leading to the waterfall. Though the spray had concealed it from a distance, here she could make out a wide, slippery-looking ledge. Was that the path they were meant to take? Did they need to go to the waterfall itself? How could they pass through such a torrent without injury? She stared up at the impressive force.

Something was splashing in the water, and the voice, which she recognized as Juni's, was making a low, rhythmic set of sounds, that to Dime, sounded ch'pyrish, like Juni was bothered by something. It was harder to hear now over the waterfall's roar.

"I think—oh no." Luja grimaced. "We have to go *under* the water." Ve went back and forth with the barely visible Juni for a while, then apparently with Stern Eyes. "Only fully under for what I think is enough to hold our breath. Then we have to go through water after that, but it sounds like we stay on the surface. Where there's air. But we have to . . . float. And still move."

Dime was surprised when Uchitar echoed her groan. "For us, it's not just about being tired. Fairies—you move in the water, right?"

"You mean swim?" Uchitar raised his brows.

"Yes." She remembered there being a landscaped pond at the Underground, down on the Heartland side. They called it *swimming*, and some fairies would do it to relax, as a soly might hike or climb. She'd learned some solies had learned to swim as well. So it was possible for everyone. Still. *In the water.* "Water is much scarcer in Sol's Reach," she explained. "We just don't do it. There are tubs, or hot tubs, but we don't propel, I mean swim, in them."

What Dime wouldn't give for a hot tub. But this wasn't the point. "Lu, you're going to have to tell them."

"Wait. Tell them I'll show you how," Uchitar said. "If they can hide, like back there, they can relax for a take. It's not hard. It's like . . . walking."

Dime was pretty sure he'd been about to say flying.

Luja talked to the newts who moved back behind a large bush, where Dime could barely see them materialize back into view, Juni still holding the branch. Dime turned back toward the shore.

Glad at least this was clear water flowing down from the jagged rocks beyond, she sighed. She hoped they wouldn't have to stay underwater long. For obvious survival reasons, but also for their clothes. Their supplies. Their bags were designed for rain, certainly not immersion. She'd wrap her notebooks and papers and food inside Batu's blanket, but that would only go so far. For now, they set the bags on the shore. Dime patted her pockets and pouches, making sure there wasn't anything that would be damaged by water.

She stopped. She had valence and a huge diamond. Couldn't she part the water, or create a giant bubble? Or float everyone in the bubble, maybe on Rosebench? She pulled Uchitar aside, asking what he thought. It was hard to talk over the roar of the waterfall. She spoke again, raising her voice.

"You could try it, but the water looks deep." He pointed. "Even if you pushed enough of that water—which I can't imagine doing—you would still sink into the water below. I guess we could all sink to the bottom first." He shuddered. "Can I just teach you swimming? Like, every ch'pyrsi who is able can do it. The newts said it was just a short distance."

"It's my bench," Rock said from behind her.

"Also, Ma-ma, I think that would be a lot of valence." She didn't realize Luja was standing beside them also. "Pyrsi would notice. They're used to your type of valence and you'd be using a lot of it. They'll feel it, specifically. Rumors would spread that someone went into the waterfall." Ve pointed to where Juni and Stern Eyes were waiting. "Theirs is different. More subtle. No, not subtle. It's emotion. We're used to it in a different way."

That was all true. If Dime were to part the river or move them through on a platform of air, this would be more than she'd ever undertaken. More, she thought, than the golden barrier she'd constructed, or the wind in the tunnels. What good would it do to sneak in from afar if someone alerted the Seats of the anomaly. Then, too, she might give away the newts' tunnel. They'd indicated few were left.

"What about the way that we fly?" she asked. "That doesn't take much. We could hold an object, like a lashed set of branches, and I could propel the object. For all of us." They'd still get wet, but at least they could move quickly.

"You could," Rock now answered. "You could also not be able to see right and run us into some sharp rock. D. Sometimes the best approach to do a thing is just to do it."

Resigned to this swimming, Dime felt silly flapping her arms around like a sea creature, her soggy clothes clinging to her like she was one. But after a few awkward flops it worked, well enough, and finally, she held her hand out toward Uchitar. He helped pull her from the water, next to Luja and Rock, who had already passed Uchitar's test or whatever this was. She gazed up at the fairy.

"Are you well?" she asked him. "I know we're pushing you too far." Now, emergency swimming lessons. She was sure he hadn't bargained on that.

"I'm fine," he said. "I'm feeling fine."

He did seem better. Though it took effort to keep his eyes alert, she expected more of the twitching and struggle she'd seen from him before. They must have caught him near the end of the worst in the prison; actually, Volana had said something along those lines.

"I think we got this," Rock said. Though, it was a bit of a question, too, as she glanced between Luja and Dime as they all dripped down onto the moss.

"Yeah," she murmured. "Thanks, Uchitar. You're a great teacher."

Her muscles already aching—she was getting too old for this—she walked up the hill to where Stern Eyes and Juni waited. She was glad to see the others had followed. "Lu, I just want to make sure they understand this will be dangerous."

"They understand, Ma-ma."

"Can you just ask them?"

Luja mumbled some stilted sounds, vis eyes fixed on vis mother.

For a stride, Dime thought Stern Eyes was going to leave. Juni stared at Dime like she was clueless.

"Don't translate that," Dime murmured to Luja. "I get it."

"Even I got that," Rock said, patting Juni's arm. Juni closed her eyes and spread her mouth wide.

Stern Eyes again talked to Luja, perhaps repeating herself, like she was coaching ver along. Luja seemed to be adjusting a little, from what Dime could tell.

"She says we are . . . sharing trust. This . . . path is a secret and must stay a secret." Ve worked back and forth a bit more. "It is a final approach, is that like a last resort maybe? Against the flying pyrsi."

"Is it me, or are they acting funny?" Rock whispered at Dime's side. "I mean, you know them. But it's like they aren't telling Lu something."

Dime thought she knew. She had a strong suspicion that from here, one could also reach Home Sha. So they were risking more than a little revealing this to a group of both Fo-ror and Ja-lal pyrsi. If they were to return to Home Sha, they could do it this way. The pyrsi living there now would be taken by surprise.

"I'll tell you later," Dime whispered back.

As Rock walked away, she worried she'd said something wrong, but tired from the new motions of swimming, she just sort of collapsed down onto the ground.

Rock returned with four small stones, not looking annoyed at all. "Light em up? It'll be dark in there. The newts know that and don't act concerned. But the rest of us, especially Lu and I, could use some light. I'm assuming it'll be pitch dark once we get through the underwater part." By Rock's shiver, she wasn't as nonchalant about that as she'd acted. "I've got some short sections of rope. We can wear them. You know, these would be great at parties."

Dime lit the stones as Rock tied quick packaging knots around each and handed them out. Uttering a quick thanks, Uchitar tied his into his hair. Luja wore vis like a large pendant, and Rock tied it around her waist, like a belt. Dime wrapped hers around a side loop of her backpack. Probably better to keep it in front, but if she were ever in need, she could make more light with her valence. Rock had to know that, so she was probably worried they might get separated. Or, back to their discussion about staying covert, she didn't want Dime lighting up their path like a glowworm.

Her stone affixed and backpack pulled tight, Dime looked to the newts. "Ask them if they would conceal themselves again." Juni still held the dead branch like a banner. "And if so, we are ready to follow."

"They said no more stopping," Luja added. Dime nodded.

She had to imagine, and perhaps the others were all thinking the same, that even if she saw the newts fade into shimmers a hundred times a turn this was not an occurrence she would get used to. Yet she tried to maintain a sense of reality as the dead branch pranced very slowly, then more steadily, along the shore, as the mist now reached them, forming into water drops on her skin. She wiped her hand across her face as they moved toward the rockface, the roar growing louder.

Dime couldn't help but think of a book she'd read as an Aoch. The details were fuzzy, as well as the actual plot, but the thing that always stood out in her mind was that the adventurers lived a while on a beautiful sheet of rock behind a waterfall. She'd always imagined the waterfall to be up in the nor mountains, but now she wondered if the author had been here.

The book had focused on comfort: a floor of smooth stone, a plateau table, soft moss, and dampened sound, with ample fruits waiting just down a safe and stunning pathway—a place young Dime had fallen asleep imagining herself in, even if a few practicalities had been overlooked. She doubted this place held such respite. From behind the torrent of spray, she could make out only darkness and sharp rocks. Even the mist on her skin felt ominous.

Would they have to pass through the falling water? No one had yet answered that. She wasn't sure pyrsi *could* do that. She tried to concentrate, as they stepped up onto the slippery ledge, each holding hands.

Before they'd edged along too terribly far, the stick before them stopped, and the others with it.

"She's saying *here*," Luja shouted, pointing through the spray. "She says you can't stand, so go fast."

They weren't to the waterfall yet, so there must be some other passage before it. "If she's going right in, we can't lose her," Dime shouted over the roar. Luja knew how fast Juni could take off, but she wanted to warn Rock and Uchitar that they may not have time to process what *here* meant. "Take a deep breath and—I don't know. Keep pushing." She and Rock met eyes.

"You go last," Rock said, hesitating. "I'll go first."

There was no time to discuss it, as the dead branch lowered into the water and then popped back up like a jumping athlete before floating away. Rock leapt right in, her cinched bag disappearing under the water. Uchitar did not hesitate either, sliding into the river with an arc to his spine and wings pulled tight behind him.

"Go," Dime mouthed, but Luja was not looking her way. Ve stepped off of the ledge, the light skin of vis scalp submerging under the roiling surface. There was nothing else to do. With a final thought to Dayn and Tum and one huge breath, Dime knelt down against the stone and tumbled ungracefully into the lake.

She opened her eyes, glad to find, as Uchitar had said, that she could still see. Propelled by her fall, she followed Luja through a sheet of slimy growth waving out from the wall, partially disrupted by the others' passage. Kicking herself downward, Dime saw a wide opening in the stone face and she pulled herself to the side, into it. Cycling her arms the way Uchitar had shown her, with her feet still flailing behind her, she wiggled and spun. *Like a toothcar,* she tried to tell herself.

But Luja was growing smaller ahead and Dime's lungs were already burning. She'd barely been in the water yet she was struggling to keep her breath held, to not give in to her desire for air, knowing there was none. Her eyes stung, and she worried what brushed against them as the disturbed water clouded before her. She tried finding ground under her feet, but the passage was already too deep, or she was too near the top, and she began to tilt and sink, instead of moving forward. Determined, she pretended she was a fish and threw her weight ahead. That helped, and she moved a stretch farther.

The exertion was making it impossible to hold her breath any longer. Maybe she could tap into some valence, just to survive long enough to make it to the others. But where would she find the air? Panic was creeping up.

Her backpack. It had saved her before. She channeled valence into her backpack and let out too much of her breath as the straps pinched her armpits, dragging her forward. Startled, she opened her mouth, and just caught herself from inhaling the water that filled it. With no more breath and panic cresting, her face ran into soft, wet feathers. She felt herself pulled upward and she drew in a huge breath, relieved that it was air, not water, that rushed in.

The idea that it could have been water filled her with terror, and she gasped, again and again, for the precious air, dangling from Juni's swaying grasp. Her light shone down from her bag, reflecting on the surface of the water in an uneven tunnel.

"Ma-ma, Ma-ma," Luja was repeating, as Rock held onto ver, one hand braced against a crag in the wall. Uchitar looked the calmest, his chest above the water and arms moving rhythmically, like he was floating.

"Dime," Rock barked, "get it together. The air seems good but we have to keep going. Everyone is fine, but we need to go."

Dime nodded, sputtering in Juni's tight grip. Juni bobbed and then, without warning, she pushed Dime forward, out of Juni's arms and back into the water. Dime felt like a kite. A crappy, wet kite being launched by a newt, she thought, as she tried to tamp down the panic inside her and think only of swimming again. Juni watched with concern until Dime imitated Uchitar's motions, the ones he'd shown her earlier to stay afloat.

Earlier, she'd thought she could help the others, but all she could do was paddle and hope and occasionally make sure she could see Luja as they made their way through the tunnel. She wasn't sure anymore where they were in relation to the waterfall, but it was clear the soft, mossy secret room of her stories was not part of this journey. The water was not rough, nor did it have a strong current. It felt like it circulated in some fashion, almost like it was breathing along with them. Their splashes echoed against the walls, and then muted as her ears sometimes dipped under the surface.

As they went, Uchitar slowed down; Dime could see Rock slowing to stay with him. The fairy knew how to swim, but Dime remembered how recently they'd carried him up that long flight of stairs, out of the same underground structure they were now approaching.

Rock was strong; she kept up fine. And, to her relief, Luja had found a rhythm up ahead, moving smoothly and even keeping vis bag above the water. Juni and Stern Eyes had no trouble; they glided along like otrips. Their biggest difficulty was the slowness of the pyrsi. Both newts were forced to stop on occasion, bobbing in the water until the others reached them. And unlike the graceful fairy, the newts struggled with keeping in place; it was easier for them to stay moving. So she tried to push.

Dime, through her exhaustion, kept feeling an itch. Almost like valence. Ah, it was valence. Inner valence. Luja was using it somehow to make verself stronger, or lighter maybe. And so when Luja drew back past the others and wrapped vis arm through one of Dime's straps, pulling her forward, Dime didn't argue. Though still moving as best she could, she was quickly running out of energy. She could have lifted her backpack again, but her underarms felt bruised from where she'd done it before.

It was a good thing Dime didn't know how much was still ahead. At each moment, she imagined them emerging into a cave or room. And then at each moment, they did not. No waterfall haven, or even a brief respite. So she persevered. She took another breath. Swung another arm. Paddled her feet. Hoped for an end. Another breath. Another arm. Another glance, to make sure Uchitar was still moving.

"Stop," Luja called. Dime started to sink, and scrambling to catch herself, her boot instead hit something. Ground. Standing. Dime knew about standing. Lurching up and checking to make sure there wasn't a ceiling in reach, she staggered to her feet, unsteady as the water swirled around her submerged legs, and more water streamed through her backpack, pulling her backward.

"I've got you," Luja said, steadying her.

"Thanks, Buttons," she murmured. Her mind and body ached to collapse but she knew they had to get to land. Hopefully this was land, not just a high point. She cringed at the thought. Ahead she saw what looked like the water's edge, lapping against the glistening stone, like the onyx beach in one of her father's stories. Ahead, the newts shook themselves dry.

As she stumbled forward, the ground turned upward, and soon the only sources of water were the streams pouring from every fabric and crevice of the pyrsi and their bags. Even if it was just a break, she had to rest. Luja let go as Dime plopped down, wincing at a sharp stone, which she brushed out from under her rear.

Juni was petting Dime's arm and she made no argument. She didn't know what Juni's rumbling meant, but it sounded sympathetic, so she reached out and ran her fingers along Juni's smooth scales. "I know, Juni."

"She says the water part is over."

"Sex with Sol," Rock wheezed.

Luja chortled.

"Check. Everyone," Dime managed to say, scooting herself against the wall. "Lu, you? Our friends?"

"They're both fine," ve said, the glowstone illuminating vis chin like an eerie tale at a campsite. "I'm fine."

"Not just from the swim. From the valence." At this point, what secrets did they have?

"I didn't go much farther than I've practiced. It's a little tingly but my mind feels ok. My arms, too. I'm fine, Ma-ma."

"Uchitar?" He hadn't yet spoken.

"I made it. And I apologize for being flap about the swimming. A round in a pond is . . . nothing like that. You all did so well."

Dime didn't think it was worth mentioning she hadn't done well at all. She'd been helplessly dragged through by a backpack, a newt, and her child. *Water part is over,* she reminded herself. Best not to think about it. Right now her only focus was on finding this place and destroying whatever Neimano kept there. "I'm just glad we're all here," she said instead. "Not *here,* but you know what I mean."

"We do," Rock said with a grin.

"I guess if you're going to grin at me like that, I don't need to check on you," she said. "I hadn't forgotten."

"I know, D. But yes, I'm fine also. Hey, though, another fairy dry-off? Or Uch, you wanna give it a roll?"

Rock seemed to regret the remark as she turned to Uchitar, who huddled to the side, his face long. Luja was staring at him.

"Alright, this direction for the dry-off," Dime said, standing and turning away from the group.

Juni almost knocked her over in excitement as she bounded through the steady wind that Dime created. Stern Eyes stayed in place and rubbed through her feathers, her head raised in a dignified manner.

Rock had no qualms, again, about making sure every angle was dry, and Luja was not shy getting right into the draft. Finally, Uchitar stood and joined them, though he just made one rotation then moved away.

Except this time, Dime was also wet, so she circled it to herself, focusing both on her clothes and directing the air gently through her backpack and the sopping pillow on top before hoisting it all back on. As the wind faded, the streams of water had stopped, and they stood now around the puddles they had made, the tunnel strangely silent.

"I hope there's another way out," Rock said, pulling out a bottle.

"What are you doing?" Dime asked, not thinking about the other piece yet. The bottle, she distracted herself. That was a fine bottle, and Dime had a good feeling where she'd got it.

"Ma-ma, stop worrying about everything," Luja said, taking the offered bottle from Rock and downing a swig.

"None for Uchitar; we've discussed it," Rock said. Uchitar nodded firmly as Rock took the bottle from Luja and held it out to Dime.

"Did you take this from fairy party dude?" She thought she saw Rock and Luja cut a sarcastic glance. That was just . . . unnecessary.

"'Take' is a rather harsh word. He wanted to supply the resistance and he gave us *full access* to said supplies."

"Rock's right." Uchitar jumped in. "He was very clear about that."

"Just give it here." Dime took a drink and was surprised that instead of some sort of burning concoction it was a lovely, bodied spirit, laced with some sort of forest flower. She had no idea what a forest flower was; she really just meant it was a perfume she couldn't quite place. "Did you get any citrus?"

It was meant as a silly question, but Rock swore under her breath as she dug out a small wrap full of cured rinds. "Not going to get out cups yet, but put this in your teeth." She handed Luja and Dime each a curved, peachy-colored rind. Dime knew she had the good teal ones in there. *Later.* She stuck it in her teeth and took another swig. Ah, that did add a nice complexity.

Juni edged over as Stern Eyes clapped her hands together. Dime tried to offer Stern Eyes a reassuring look. "No, Juni, I'm sorry. Lu, tell her I have no idea how old she is, as in whether a cub is like an actual ch'pyr. Also, I have no idea if this would harm her. Blame me. Tell her I said no."

Stern Eyes howled out a few additional words that felt strongly like agreement, and whether Juni was listening to her or to Dime, she slunk into a shadow.

After handing it one more time to Luja—Dime tried not to get wrapped up about it—Rock worked in a stopper and put the bottle back in her bag, which she hefted back on.

"Are we ready to do this?" she asked.

Dime wasn't sure. Uchitar was wringing his hands, Juni was sulking in the corner, and Stern Eyes picked through her feathers. It was Luja, the glowstone hanging from vis neck, that stepped forward.

"Let's go," ve said.

Interlude

Some pyrsi judged Catatiana for getting away from Pito, but she'd stopped caring about that long ago. For one, they weren't here. More importantly, they didn't know anything about why she'd needed to leave.

She didn't owe anyone an explanation.

Her rations had decreased, and she had to cart the deliveries herself, from far upforest. Still didn't care. Enjoying the scent of minerals wafting on the breeze, she stretched out on a long stone and stared out at the delta, the old tablecloth underneath her a nice shield from the heat. Her needles were nestled back into her bag. She'd deal with them in a bit.

The delta was the one place pyrsi hadn't yet messed up, the way Catatiana saw it. Disliked by pyrsi and larger animals for the lack of solid ground, she'd pledged to live here with humility—her own way, but not disturbing the beauty that was. If this was where small animals found safety, even better. Now she was small too.

A host of creatures flew, jumped, and bounded across the murky water. A family of otrips played in the mud—the young ones digging and leaping while the parent searched for food.

The delta food wasn't bad, she'd learned. Bitter berries could be softened and buds and twigs held rich flavor. The sticky weeds cleaned up nice and had a pleasant, chewy texture and a savory depth a pyr couldn't find in the finest city joints.

She didn't mind the muddy water, either. Sure, the rushing

shores of Sha were exciting, at least had been before so many of them were blocked off. Pools, lakes, and waterfalls were spectacular, but they were crowded and belonged to a world that Catatiana had left now. She'd had to.

Rivers and streams flowed like music, and she couldn't fault a pyr for enjoying one.

Pyrsi needed water. And even if the high-class folks took all the good spots, she'd learned there was water everywhere. Everywhere that had a short rain, or the blessings of a clean faucet, or even a little outdoor rain-catcher, one for the birds. Maybe a painting of water, or a song that reminded one of it. A cup of drinking water. A memory. Memories could be vivid as the present, if a pyr gave them a little space to bloom.

Tears. Tears were water too. Everyone she knew had those.

Catatiana had a lone shelter on the far reaches of the delta. A small, disrespectable home, run over by critters and often requiring an extra wash. That was fine.

A hollow *plunk* interrupted her thoughts, as something too fast for her eyes had found a deep spot and dove in, little rings giving away xyr path. Dried leaves swept from a nearby branch, and skittered, stopped, and started again, as they made their way down, toward Sha.

A slow tune escaped under her breath, and she began to hum along, louder now. Then, into full song. A blue-striped bird stopped, tilting xyr scruffy head as if to say that wasn't so bad for a pyr. Another landed nearby, tufts of orange and red feathers pinned to xyr head like a fancy hat. Seeing each other, the two started, and each hopped back.

Birds liked their space. And so did she.

She continued to sing and to her great delight, a small cloud passed by, sprinkling a small wave of rain across the bent trees, the spotted mud, and the lines of flowing water. It swept on, across her, and her tablecloth, and over the feathers of the watching birds.

Leaning back, she relished the drops of water on her face, letting them sink into her wandering hair and into her worn clothes.

Sometimes it was hard to get to a spot alone—whatever that spot was—and take a moment to relax. And one might not have a spot like this. Still, she hoped wherever a pyr was, whatever spot xe did have, xe'd remember to take a flap or two there.

And find xemself by the water.

Act 2

Darkness

"**We couldn't have** taken care of this xemself?" Rock grumbled as they picked and wove through the passage. "What sort of agent is xe? Why are we cleaning up xyr mess? And that is not getting into the creepy room and simply unnecessary shadow talk." Despite careful attention to her handholds, she managed to waggle a finger back. "Neimano did this a full two epochs ago, and the best the Seats did was assign a pyr to *know* about it. Sort of. And now we've got to crawl in here."

"Your government in action," Dime replied. Then, remembering this was the Fo-ror government they were complaining about this time, she turned back to Uchitar.

Luja nearly ran right into her, and behind, Juni barked.

"Sorry!" Dime said.

"You can't just slow down like that, Ma-ma."

"I said I was sorry. Anyway, I was looking for Uchitar. I just hope it's fine that we're grumbling a little."

"I'm grumbling a little," she thought she heard Rock say.

Dime saw Uchitar was listening and continued on. "I know the Fo-ror don't talk about the Seats like this. We're a little more open about our Circles. But if you're uncomfortable we can stop."

"Now she's apologizing for me," Rock said from ahead. "Uch knows I'm just letting steam. *Pffft.*"

Dime was pretty sure fairies knew what steam was.

"It's ok," Uchitar said, his voice flat. "Somewhere between my stints in prison and spending time with all of you, I've stopped worrying about the Seats' sanctity."

"That's great," Rock said with a little whistle, "'cause right now, I'm not feeling like a huge fan."

"Besides, that's the whole point of the Foundry," he added. "To talk about it. We've all agreed not to talk outside of the meetings, but you know, seems private enough here."

"Indeed. Aw, harm," Rock grumbled, her foot slipping on loose gravel. She caught herself, managing to stay upright.

So far, the tunnel had been a long, singular stretch, without forks. That was one less thing to deal with for now. What concerned her was that they were going downhill. Not wanting to further worry the group—well, she was sure Rock was thinking it—she kept her thoughts to herself. But this bothered her for three primary reasons. One, she'd learned a long time ago that when you take a nice, easy walk downhill, you are bound to have to go uphill later. Second, they'd just emerged from water not long ago. Would they encounter more water, moving downward? Or was the water just a factor of being near the river earlier? Third, it was just . . . awful. Like plunging into the depths of the land looking for wickedness. It wasn't an appealing idea as a metaphor, let alone literally.

She supposed there was a reason pyrsi built into the trees and towers and mountains. Perhaps it was why they wore heels.

Oh, and air quality. That was clearly a fourth thing, though Dime was taking the counting way too far. Dayn always said she did; maybe he had a point.

The newts' presence reassured her. She knew they wouldn't lead the group to danger, and figuring especially that Juni had saved her twice, she'd trust her friend with her and her child's life. Not that Juni needed to prove anything; she was just making the point. To herself. In her thoughts.

She sighed, moving on.

Suddenly, their lights seemed to fade, but it wasn't the light that changed, it was the space. Dime knew, inherently, that whatever the larger set of tunnels and caves in the center of Ada-ji was, they had now made their way to it. No diamonds here, but patterned walls, in shades of dark red and a slate blue. At first she thought the patterns were natural lines of stone, but a few appeared intentional.

She didn't have a name for this place. It was part passages, part rooms, part crags and ledges. A cavern, she supposed, though with many layers. At least there was air, swirling through, punctuated by distant drips of water.

That party pyr, he'd had a view of the canopy. She hoped she could see the treetops again, someday.

Juni was squealing to her side, and Stern Eyes tapped Juni's upper back, chattering in what Dime couldn't decide were calming or scolding tones.

"They hear the machines," Luja said. "I can . . . hear them too. If I listen."

"I need to learn this stuff," Rock added. Dime knew she was talking about solies' inner valence, which should be within Rock's abilities as well as Luja's.

Dime's valence was the same as Uchitar's, and she looked over to see his reaction, but he was staring off at the wall. She started to walk over to him, but she tripped over a sharp rock, yelping. Luja reached out, and she took vis arm.

Maybe a little more light.

She tossed some valence out, not to flood the space but enough, just now, to see what they were dealing with.

Normally, Stern Eyes' and Juni's reactions were as different as their temperaments, but surprisingly they both shouted and spun, scanning the walls and ceiling. Was it her valence? Should she not have—

"It's different," Luja said. "It's . . . broken. No, maybe damaged. Look, look up."

She tried to see what they were saying, as the newts' uproar dwindled to murmurs.

"Yeah, look, D." Rock was pointing. "It's not like what we saw in the caves before. Much, much worse. Cracks and fragments, both tiny and sizeable." She closed her eyes, concentrating. "Oh, I feel it now, too. Harmed-off Boring Project." She turned her finger toward Uchitar. "This is for you, Uch, for disrespecting your Seats earlier." She stood taller. "The killbringing Circles can send their righteous authorities to ... whatever room is under this one ... for being so *full of shit* that they would put pyrsi's lives at risk when pyrsi *told* them they were doing so. *A flock of harmbirds on their picnic space.*"

"Is it better?" Dime asked.

Even Luja had stepped back, letting go of Dime.

"It's not better. I'm pissed." She cinched up her bag, and Dime noticed a new stream of water leaking out onto the floor. Dime took some valence and tried to draw it out, without putting Rock's inventory at risk. The bag rose, as if lightened.

Oddly, Uchitar laughed, but otherwise didn't respond.

Luja peered across, and then upward. "Stern Eyes said this area has changed. There have been rock falls, I guess. They seem a little confused which way to go." Ve moved closer to Dime. "I'll say this since they can't understand me when I talk without emotion. Juni has definitely not been here before, and I'm almost wondering if Stern Eyes has either. It feels like they are dealing more with passed-down knowledge. So I think that explains how upset they are. And how shocked."

Dime considered how anyone could pass down complex geographical knowledge without records or maps. Yet, she believed that they did. And pyrsi were supposed to be the advanced ones.

"Yeah, they're confused," Luja continued. "They say the path through the waterfall was there and mostly correct, but this isn't what they expected."

Dime remembered her wrist compass, and she set her bag down, trying to find it. The needle skipped a little, but gave an indication where the concentration of diamonds was. She knew as they grew closer, it would grow more erratic. Maybe it could help for now. She buckled it over her wrist.

"Work gift," she explained, turning it toward Rock.

"Work gift? What in Ada-ji are you talking about."

"My friends in the IC gave it to me. At the party after my last shift. The same turn the High Guards showed up. They thought it was a compass that pointed nor/sur, but it actually points toward the diamond mines. Ugh, diamond caves, I mean."

She'd forgotten she used to call them mines. All the solies did. Except, they were spoken of as a myth, or an abstraction maybe. Sometimes, like pyrsi weren't hearing the words they were saying. They were just used to saying them.

"It points to diamonds?" Uchitar had almost disappeared in the shadows. "That's fascinating."

"Yeah," Dime answered. "It took me a while to figure that out. I kept thinking it was broken."

Rock *tsked*, her mouth twisting to one side. "So the IC gave you a going away party before they escorted you to the curb and continued to operate like you never existed, but before you left they gave you a gift that would help lead you to the largest source of power on Ada-ji, except we can't give them credit for this, because they probably got it in some antique shop to help you take toothcars to the market. And that's if it wasn't a regift." She'd placed a hand on her hip.

"Maybe they meant it as a metaphor for life. Or just know that I like small gadgets and thought I would enjoy something unique."

"Maybe. Or it's both, and they were signaling that they thought you were turning your life into a small gadget."

"Whatever! They cared. Someone went to a shop for this."

"Maybe," Rock repeated.

Dime shook her head. "Look. I hear you, but it might be handy." She stared down at the smudged glass face. "Eh. If we have any big decisions, I'm using Ador's dice." The thought had popped out.

She'd received both within a few bells, now that she thought about it. "Ador gave me this lovely pair of stone dice, right before it all happened," she explained to Uchitar. She'd almost said *my friend* but then recalled Uchitar and Ador had met, at the den.

"They're actually your dice if he gave them to you," Luja suggested.

"It's shorthand." Had she taught her kid to be as literal as she was? Sol, she'd have to work on that. "Besides, I like thinking of them as Ador's. Remembering the friends I have comforts me." She rested a hand over the dial, then lifted it. An image of Jenn came to mind. She wondered what ve was doing now.

Stern Eyes had sat down and was picking at her feet, but Juni was making rather indignant gestures, pointing between herself and Stern Eyes.

"Hold on," Luja muttered. "We can't leave them out." They all waited as ve stumbled through explaining their conversation.

Without permission, Juni lifted Dime's arm, turning it as she gazed at the small device.

At this point . . .

"Do you have one of those pre-cut rope segments? The soft ones?" Rock would know she was referring to the same segments they'd used to tie the glowstones.

As Rock pulled one from her bag, Dime removed the compass from her wrist. She added the rope as an extension, but then remembered Stern Eyes was there and she was almost doing it again. "Luja, can I give this to . . . without it being taken as a leader-gift?"

After a brief exchange, Stern Eyes almost looked blasé. "She says that things that used to feel important don't feel important now," Luja said. "I think seeing the cracks in the caves is really bothering her."

It should be. Not wanting to send this through translation, Dime sat next to the older of the two newts. She leaned over and pressed herself against Stern Eyes, letting the weight of her body speak for her.

Stern Eyes rustled her talons through Dime's hair, and while Dime braced for rough contact, her touch was soft. Comforting. She was glad they understood each other.

Dime rose and walked back to Juni, who howled in delight as she realized what Dime was doing. With the compass fixed around Juni's arm, the newt jumped in place, turning each time until a circle had been completed. Then she stopped, a guttural noise emerging. That didn't sound as happy. Dime wasn't ready to deal with something big. Not yet.

Luja glanced over. "It's the boring, the vibration of the drills through the stone. We can all feel it. It feels—" ve ran vis hands over vis arms as though cold "—harmful."

"Which way?" Uchitar's words were blunt, but yes, they needed to keep moving. Perhaps he was right to stay disconnected. There would be time later to chat. She hoped.

Walking turned out to be not the right word for it. Unlike the passage before, there wasn't a smooth path to follow. There were ridges, and steps, and even large breaks in the rock. Breaks that were not old. Dayn had told her, during their last discussion on the subject, that the drilling itself wasn't usually the cause of damage or instability.

"The land reacts like a living being," he'd said. "When you are poked by a thorn, you might twitch. And when you twitch, you might bump something else. When bumped, you could fall. Once fallen, you could despair. Some pieces of you might remain strong, and others transfer weakness like a vein."

Dime had been surprised at the normally direct Dayn for being so allegorical, but she was starting to understand why. For a pyr who'd spent his life analyzing the structures that gave pyrsi a place to live, a place to feel safe, it must have been distressing to feel them shudder and creak and react—like a hurt creature, with no one caring. *Vein*, he'd said. Like the land lived.

The CC had seemed like a structural and unemotional place to work, unlike the flow of emotion that Luja, for example, would experience in the medical enclaves. Yet, what if an expert viewed each building, each wall, each layer of stone as the body that held the life of Ada-ji?

She wondered where he was now. He'd stayed back at the Underground, studying the rocks and tunnels there, to the eas. Was he standing somewhere in the depths of Ada-ji right now, staring up as she was, lamenting the rumbling overhead?

I miss you, she told him.

Eventually Dime could hear the drilling sounds too, and even feel the tremble as she reached for new handholds. Whether from recent or previous changes, each cavern or section brought new rockfalls, or large cracks or steps that needed to be traversed. One section was so hard to pass, she and Rock had to get out their climbing gear, and take turns sharing it with Luja. Uchitar had found space to use his wings, and thank Sol the newts had been large enough to clamber across.

Even if Dime could figure a way to use valence, she knew that as they neared the complex, the risk of being detected would increase. Yet, sometimes, as they walked and climbed, she rested her hand over her pendant.

No one discussed it, but they must all also be thinking the obvious—if there had already been cave-ins, might there not be more? They weren't safe here.

The farther inward they traveled, the more Dime had to remind herself that it wasn't really such a long distance; they'd started in the city of Pito, after all, even if the city was large. It just felt like a long distance, with all the obstacles and darkness.

This didn't prevent a broader feeling of isolation from setting in; at some point, she felt like they were traveling so far that they would never find a way out. A hollowness grew in her chest and she tried to ignore it, to focus on her friends. Yet the newts even, so sure they could find their way into the caves, walked with an uneasy gait, exchanging low moans that Luja either didn't know how to translate, or wouldn't.

Her thoughts grew darker, and she even considered that if they were trapped here, at least Volana knew where they went. At least she could tell Dayn.

Uchitar was tapping his elbows, and Rock was talking to herself. They couldn't go on like this.

"What's your favorite part of carpentry?" she asked Uchitar. Dime didn't think it was a sensitive subject. It had been one topic that had raised his spirits in the past.

"The smell."

She hadn't expected that.

"I know I'm supposed to say the satisfaction of helping pyrsi or the long-lasting structures that wear and age like friends, but I love the smells. Not just cut wood, but old wood and dried moss. Saps and waters. I even enjoy the smells of oil and varnish. It smells deep, and clean, and—"

He stopped, tapping a low patch of ceiling. His tenor shifted. "It's so hard to move in here. I'm used to flying over things. I don't know how to climb." Uchitar's fingers looked swollen and raw; Dime had found him kitchen gloves in Pyrilee's storage—one thing the fairy space was missing was climbing gear—but he said they made his fingers sweat and kept taking them off.

"That's interesting, you know," Dime offered, trying to keep the conversation moving. "We felt the same about swimming. You're used to swimming, but we're used to climbing. Makes you wonder how many things we think are difficult simply because we haven't tried them."

Here, she thought this was an interesting thought, but no one had any response. She looked behind at Luja, but ve didn't acknowledge her. Rock was muttering again. And Uchitar had gone from nervous to excited to upset over a few sentences. The newts continued to grumble and didn't seem to want to communicate for now with the pyrsi. Stern Eyes was fixed on sniffing and listening, and Juni kept checking the wrist compass, grunting to it as she walked.

Dime felt a surge from the distant drills, this time vibrating in her feet, even so slightly. It didn't make sense. Why had they restarted now, when as far as she could tell, they'd stopped ever since—

Oh, harm.

"Rock." She edged up closer to her, not wanting to get into the details of this story with everyone else. "Rock."

"I feel them," she muttered, not looking back.

"No, I just realized. In the caves. When I— Your injury." She pushed away the image of Rock's sliced skin. The blood. Dime had thought her uncontrolled burst of valence had only broken the column that had injured Rock. What if she'd done more?

Now Rock stopped. She spun around. The others continued to trudge forward.

"Are you saying you did stop them after all? Is that possible? I mean, think how far we had to be from those drills. What could you even have done?"

"Yes, I mean, *harm*—we've seen that my valence can be pretty impactful when I'm emotional and not thinking about it. I was so upset by the idea that the Circles, that I supported all those cycles, could be putting the Fo-ror at risk that I think something zapped out of me. The same thing that cut the ceiling."

Not her most elegant description, but the idea had her terrified. The crack she'd made outside of the city had haunted her thoughts, the sight of it repeating at unknown noises or unwanted thoughts. Yet, if she did damage the boring machines, then she was capable of harming things she couldn't even see? What if pyrsi had been hurt? Dizzying ripples ran from her chest into her nose, and she tried to breathe through them. If the drills had been harmed, Sala would have heard, right? Especially if pyrsi had been hurt. Except the modified operation was a secret from Sala. Maybe they didn't tell Sala. Maybe it hadn't been just Rock she hurt that turn, and maybe—

"Hey!" Rock was right near her. "You can't freak out."

"Why can't I? I caused harm through layers of stone and dirt to something I couldn't even see, at the same time I injured you. Who knows who else I injured. You don't know. I don't know. Don't you see? *I'm* the Violence. I'm the one we should all be protected from."

"Harm it, D, stop right now. Let me tell you something. I'm not that young agent you once knew. Just as you became a manager and a mother and started a whole Solharmed revolution—don't argue with me—I've grown and learned too. And one thing I've done is spent a whole career watching good folks pick apart their every move while pyrsi who don't give a single heartbeat do whatever they want and don't suffer from the stress."

She reached out her hands and Dime barely realized that she took them.

"I don't know if it's your fault. I don't know if you made a mistake. But I'm not going to stand here and watch you berate yourself over unknowns when you are doing your best to grow, to bring light to the world and more importantly, to the pyrsi around you." She stopped, Dime avoiding her gaze. "You know, we keep talking about paynotes and fairies and high class pyrsi with party homes, and all I've been able to think is maybe our resources should be distributed based on how much a pyr *cares*." Rock let go, and Dime's hands swung back to her side.

"How could you measure that?"

"We measure the work we do now, and there are always basic rights. It's like you said earlier, and yes I was listening, maybe we think things are difficult because we haven't tried them. We—"

The others had stopped and were calling back. Exchanging a look, they hurried to catch up.

"We're fine," Dime called. "Sorry, we were discussing something." She tried to refocus on their path.

Everyone had returned to their thoughts, and Dime tried to ignore the burn in her limbs as they moved along. If hers felt such fatigue, she couldn't imagine how Uchitar's felt. He pressed on without complaint but with notable shifts in mood. At one point, she'd thought she'd heard him crying. Not sure what to do, she'd offered him some water, and asked if he needed anything.

Luja seemed to be keeping an eye on him. She could see, though, why Volana found this so stressful.

She scanned the area, brightening her glowstone as the light flickered around the space. The ground was smoother than the other sections, with a long slope and dark expanse to one side. "We should eat and rest," she suggested.

Rock set down her bag. "Pee over here," she said, walking off toward a steeper drop-off.

Luja conversed with Juni and Stern Eyes, who, to Dime's surprise, didn't argue, but went to follow Rock.

Dime wriggled her bag to the ground, groaning at the soreness in her shoulders. She was glad to stop for many reasons, one that, with the largest bag, she'd taken a lot of the food herself. Unloading some would take a bit of the weight off her back. Her legs wobbled as she sat down. Slowly, she stretched forward then released.

She allowed herself to throw a little light to the ceiling, which she scanned for anything that might fall, and then she set out what she couldn't help but think a rather gloomy picnic. Forget that. Thinking of Tum, she started humming one of her child's favorite songs, trying to stay cheerful. After all, the darkness wasn't everything.

Except, in here, it was.

Dime loved the night. Unlike Batu's preference for day, nighttime had always been her preferred side of a turn. But this wasn't night. This was darkness. Isolation. Fear. That was different.

Nighttime was openness and air and peace and beautiful, beautiful dark with the reassurance that Sol would take vis turn and depart again. Dime floated a bag of dried berries onto the ground, with Juni not waiting to dig in. She scooped a handful of the berries through her talons and then nearly smashed them against her teeth. Stern Eyes clicked something from the side. Rock was back as well.

"Have you thought about how recently you learned you have valence and now you're casually using it?" It was Luja who spoke.

Dime had to count a little, as the events had become hazy. She and Rock had gone into the diamond caves at night, apparently when she'd damaged the drills. Then, she'd been at the den. The next nighttime had held the speech at commons. Uchitar had been there. That's right; Rock had been too. Then she'd been at the Underground. A much nicer underground than this one. Then at Batu's. Then this last long night, where they'd removed Uchitar from prison and she'd found Rock again. So five turns? Less than six turns since she'd even used valence, intentionally anyway, and now she was throwing it about?

But what about Luja? Luja had learned about inner valence after Dime had returned from the caves, and ve didn't have a huge diamond to assist ver along. Though, ve did have intact heart tissue. Yet . . . her child was in much the same situation, using valence within six turns of knowing it even existed.

Dime needed to stop thinking she was so different. "At this point, maybe everyone has it. Who's left, kitas?"

Luja grew quiet.

"I don't even want to know."

She ignored Rock's chuckle. That's right, Rock had met Agni too, at the Beds. That was so recently. Again, it all felt hazy. Dime just wanted normal turns. Even for a while.

Inspired by her hosts' careful hospitality over those same turns she'd just considered, Dime worked to set out a meal that felt inviting.

"Angles always help," she said to Luja. "Look, if I put this pretzel stick here, aligned with the trays, it looks boring. If I *tilt* it—" she moved each to an angle "—now it looks fancy. You don't need paynotes to be fancy," she lectured. "Just care and small details." She paused. "But you do need them for the food."

At that moment, Juni ran up and grabbed one of the pretzel sticks. Then she held it out, as if asking for Dime's permission.

"Sure, Juni." The newt crunched through the stick, sending a spray of crumbs onto Dime's neatly arranged display. Fine; fancy wasn't going to happen.

"Hey, the company is great." Rock gave Dime a kind smile that she couldn't help but return.

Yet, Rock was rummaging in her own bag. "D, make a little valence fire, right here." She pointed to a flat piece of stone.

Dime started to argue, but seeing Rock's face, she sighed. With a flick of her finger, she lit a small flame.

Juni jumped, and as Dime worried that the newt's head might hit the ceiling—though it wasn't even close—she jumped herself as Juni started dancing, happily, on the cavern floor. "Tell her not to touch it," Dime warned Luja. "And we can't keep it on too long, because of the smoke." Dime realized she could waft the smoke away if needed. Still, good to be safe.

Humming along as happily as the newt, Rock clanked together some sort of thin metal contraption, shaped almost like a warped . . . construction cone on a plate? What was she doing? Rock wriggled a pipe into it, then sat a big brown brick on top of a saucer-like thing. Finally, she popped out some sort of flat metal scraper.

Luja and Juni clapped in delight. Uchitar edged over to see as Stern Eyes peered over with either skepticism or annoyance. Dime nodded at her, and was glad she returned what Dime thought was a nod of agreement.

The dark brick began to melt and run down the sides of the item. "What the harm is that?" Dime finally asked. Everyone ignored her. "Wait . . . is that a coco fountain? How do you have a coco fountain? We are supposed to be in peril."

"Did anyone else find it amusing to be intensely raiding a party pad for mission supplies? I did, and I found this coco fountain."

"How are we going to clean that?"

Rock sighed. "We're sleeping, right? We enjoy it now, it cools while we sleep, we crack off any remaining coco, and then we move on our way." She sat up. "D, this place is pretty dismal. We could use some coco. And if I get some shreds in the bottom of my bag, I will survive it. This cavey world will not argue, and my bag's already endured being soaked in river water."

Once Dime saw Luja turning vis pretzel stick into the melting coco, she gave up and scooched in. The warmed coco was soft and bittersweet against the hard, salty pretzel and Dime knew, in this case, there was no need to tell Rock she was awesome.

"Uchitar, do you want any?" He was sitting to the back, his legs bouncing a bit.

"Don't push him," Luja whispered. "Better for him to eat calming foods." Well, Lu would know best what he needed at this stage of his recovery. Dime did make sure, again, he had plenty of water, and she served him a disproportionate amount of the still-fresh bread.

"Thanks," he said, offering her a warm smile.

She sat next to him.

He took a bite of the bread. The others were eating theirs plain, but Dime had poured some flame-heated dal-gravy over hers and let it soak in. A bite proved that was a good decision.

"Thanks for coming with us," Dime replied, in a break between chewing.

"You must miss your spouse," he said.

"I do." Dime stared ahead. "We've been apart so much lately, I almost try not to think about him now. When I do . . . it overwhelms me. We've . . . been through a lot together, even before all this. I don't want to be all like 'he's my life' like I don't have my own, but I couldn't imagine a road forward where we weren't hand in hand. We're . . . friends.

"Sorry," she uttered. "I'm just . . . holding a lot. I didn't mean to get so intense."

Uchitar didn't answer; he had turned away. She knew he'd had great difficulties with his own family, so maybe she shouldn't have talked about Dayn. But he'd asked. She thought quickly.

"I also don't see a road where *we* aren't friends," she said to the turned ma'pyr. "If you'll have me."

Uchitar stood quietly and walked off into the darkness, leaving his food half-finished. Dime didn't see his glowstone, but he could turn his on and off with valence. Respecting his privacy, she pushed up with a slight groan, and walked back to the group. She rubbed her hands together, as the floor was quite dirty.

"What do you think Ador and Volana are doing right now?" she mused.

"Volana might still be asleep." Rock didn't seem to be making a joke. "After that, after seeing how she made party pyr put his . . . resources where his ego was . . . I bet she'll go back to the Foundry and be shy no more."

"Ador is doing what he's always done," Luja added.

Dime knew ve didn't mean it as an insult, but she didn't know if ve knew how much of a compliment that was. It had taken Dime longer to understand. She couldn't fret over that, but she now had a deeper appreciation of someone who'd weathered these storms a really long time, even when he sometimes stood alone.

"Have you ever thought about what makes a good leader?" Dime had the sudden question. She thought she knew.

"Humility?" Luja offered.

"Nope," Rock replied. "I mean I think you're on the right track, but I pyrsonally believe some balance of self is healthy. Too humble can be sort of a show, you know?"

"You're too much of a skeptic," Dime joked, as Rock ignored her. She took a seat, turning to see Uchitar had joined them. He rested a quick hand on Dime's shoulder—Dime had given him permission to touch her, but Fo-ror always forgot Ja-lal shirts had padded shoulders—before lowering down.

"I'd like that," was all he said, his hands now folded over his leg. Dime rested a hand over them, pulling it back awkwardly. They were rather cold.

To the side, Stern Eyes nearly clucked at him, and Juni scooted closer until he leaned in for a hug. It was nice to see the fairy and newt in deep embrace. She relaxed back against the wall.

"Compassion," Rock said. "Connectedness. A leader needs to make decisions, and they need to ask for input. And you can't do both of those things right if you don't feel your place in the fabric. Not—" she pointed "—under it."

"Ok, sage." Dime was glad to see Rock looked amused. "Who's the best leader you've ever met?"

"Volana will be," she said, taking a giant bite of bread dipped in coco. The tin of mints was resting, open, in front of her. "Watch that one."

"Of course I agree," Uchitar said, his gaze distant.

"Da-da is a good leader," Luja answered. "He defers to you a lot, but you should see him when you're not there."

Dime didn't know what that meant. Ella had been on her mind, but Ella had lived her life, these last cycles, alone. Luja was saying something to the newts. They shifted uncomfortably.

"I offended them," ve said with a sigh. "I asked what they thought, trying to include them, but it doesn't work that way. It always comes back to who has the best name." Ve crossed vis arms.

Juni looked much less offended a stride later, with Stern Eyes scolding her for having dipped her mouth in the pool of coco, where it was now cooling onto her face. She did look happy, though. Dime almost did it herself. Instead she took the mint Rock offered her and popped it into her mouth, realizing she hadn't actually tried one yet. The taste was subtler than she'd expected, and she sat back and turned the small candy in her teeth as it dissolved.

She glanced around at their odd group. Each seemed, for a few takes, to leave to a different place. She wondered what each was thinking, including her child. Dime was thinking how lucky she was to have them.

They finished the meal, trying to save some of the water they'd brought. She and Rock got out the compact blankets Batu had made them and untied the pillows from their bags, glad they felt dry and hoping they wouldn't smell too much like the lake. Uchitar and Luja wriggled out the blankets they'd each taken from the party place.

"Didn't you bring pillows?"

"Not enough room," Luja said with a yawn. "Figured water better filled the space."

"You share mine," she said. "Or have it. I'll be fine."

"No, it's ok. I've got a plan. Uchitar, a stride?"

Luja sat with Uchitar a take, and Dime figured Volana had told ver how to best care for him. She got her own bed together, as she chatted back and forth with Rock. Slowly, she adjusted the pillow, which was more comfortable than she'd assumed after its earlier dousing.

And still, Dime did not expect when Juni and Luja curled up together, Luja nestling vis head onto Juni's side.

Uchitar did not grab a newt, but he insisted he was fine.

And Dime, with a final wave, turned off the light across the ceiling.

Neimano walked in, bellowing a deep laugh. Dime sat up from her blanket, noticing the others were gone.

"I arrested them," he said through his laughter.

Who else had been here? She couldn't quite remember.

"What makes you hurt pyrsi?" she asked, stumbling for what she could say. Why was she here? Something was wrong, she knew. "Why would anyone want to harm? The idea chills my soul. Yours? It doesn't?"

Neimano didn't answer. He pulled a bubbling glass vessel from his pocket, the green liquid glowing in the darkness of the cave. It *blooped* and *bleeped* with enthusiastic sounds and Neimano smiled down at it.

"You don't care," she murmured. "You don't care at all."

The glassware continued to grow in his hands, but he held it forward, effortlessly. Around the room, faces came into view. Hundreds, maybe thousands of pyrsi, watching him from the shadows.

Dayn burst in, gripping a huge, curved blade. "Don't touch her," he said. "Don't touch my Diamond."

"My Diamond. My Diamond!" the towering fairy hissed.

"You don't care!" She turned around, scanning the faces. They were blurry, and she couldn't tell if they were Ja-lal or Fo-ror. "You care," she implored. "You do, right? Don't you care?" she shouted, now, as loudly as she could.

"Dayn," she called, wishing she could hold him. Wishing he'd drop that blade.

"*Kill him!*" a voice demanded. She realized xe was talking to Dayn, whose blade had also grown to counter the huge green vessel. And the pyrsi around, their fingers crackled with valence, with more blades shining somehow in the lack of light.

"No," Dime whispered. "No." She pulled from the arms holding her, but they did not let go.

"Ma-ma," the voice said, softly. "Ma-ma."

Sitting up, Dime gazed into pure darkness, confused. She lit her glowstone and it illuminated Luja's concerned face.

"They are still sleeping," ve whispered. "Except Stern Eyes. She was the one who woke me. You're having a dream. We're still here. We're here with you."

Dime leaned into Luja's arms, feeling awkward as she drew from the strength of the Aoch.

"It's ok," ve said, as if understanding. Ve pulled her in. Tighter.

Releasing her, ve patted the blanket and pillow. "Juni's up too, now. But they will go back to sleep. And you should, too. Will you be well? Or should I sit here?"

Confused, but starting to grasp where she was, Dime murmured, "Thank you. I think I'll be ok."

"I'll be here if you need me," her child said.

Comforted, Dime drifted back to sleep.

Rock hummed a tune as she scraped the coco film off the cool metal, cracking off little pieces and plunking them into the decorative tin. If she had heard Dime's unrest, she'd kept it to herself. Luja's bag was set and ready to go, and Juni and Stern Eyes were picking through each other's feathers, an act of friendship Dime was relieved not to share. Uchitar sat to the side, but he seemed to be managing. It must be hard, traveling alone. Everyone else here had someone familiar.

Rock had risen and was holding out a small white object. "It's a tooth cube," she was saying, showing it to Luja. "Look, you just rub it in your mouth and then scrub your finger around. It's bubbly and everything. Good stuff. No jar."

Ve hesitated.

"Occasionally you're just like your mother," Rock said. "I grabbed a whole set of them; I was *not* suggesting that we share." She tossed one of the small cubes to Luja, who caught it with a grin. One more to Uchitar, who kept it but didn't react.

"Sure!" Rock said, Dime not sure to whom. Soon two more cubes were zipping through the air, caught with certainty by Juni and Stern Eyes.

"Tell them don't eat it," Rock added. "Tell them, scrub only. Then, uh, leave it here." She shrugged at Dime. "They're natural, and I'm not putting used ones in my bag. Except my *own*."

The newts sniffed the cubes, then began to scrub vigorously, first at their teeth, then across the pads of their hands and feet, and then into the crack of their rears. Juni snorted.

"See?" Rock said, holding out a final cube.

Recognizing that she had the strangest and best group of friends in all of Ada-ji, Dime accepted one of the tooth squares, put it into one of her now empty food wrappers, put her bag back on, and set out. She'd use it later. After she'd unseen that a bit.

The ache in her muscles walked with her at this point, as did the dread of what their group might find. Now that they'd rested from the effects of traveling through the water and that first difficult stretch, she didn't think they'd want to risk resting again.

This was it.

They moved on. Sometimes they'd find a smooth passage and be able to walk with more certainty and comfort. Other times, they'd encounter piles of rubble or shifted ground, and need to improvise their way through.

Luja and Rock seemed to maintain their strength, but Dime was feeling another ache, one she knew was more mental than physical. She felt unwell. Having to constantly think about the Violence was a massive drain on her being. But would it be right to ignore it? Uchitar looked similarly affected. Where he'd had energy for a while, his wings now drooped and he sometimes tripped over his steps. She moved up next to him, offering an encouraging nod, which he returned with a tight smile.

The compass told them they were still generally going the right way, so Dime tried not to worry about which specific path to take. She did make good on her pledge and used Ador's dice a few times when they weren't sure. Though still faint, the rumbling echoes from the drills grew more noticeable, and a new sensation arose also: the diamonds. Now that she was closer, they drew her. She did not tell the others this, but simply stated her own votes with more confidence than she had before, and without looking at Juni's wrist.

"This way," she said. "I feel sure."

Stern Eyes nodded along with each declaration, and Dime started to wonder if she could feel it too. If Dime hadn't spoken up, would Stern Eyes now be leading them the same way?

A loud thump sounded behind her.

Uchitar had fallen and rolled onto his side. His whole body trembled and he moaned in agony. Dime rushed over, fumbling to find her flask.

Luja was already there, prying open his eyelids with vis fingers. "*Killblade*, I knew it." From vis half-seat, half-kneel, ve waved an arm around at the others, and barked something at the newts, who stepped immediately back. "Don't touch him," ve commanded.

Except ve was touching him, running vis hands down his legs and under his arms until ve stopped, prying vis fingers into a seam and ripping the threads loose. Pulling out a wrap of paper between two fingers, ve spread it out onto one palm and unfolded it, revealing a light-colored powder.

Dime's heart jumped. She'd never seen tzetz before. That had to be what this was.

"I don't want to hear it," ve said, eyes set. "Just help me."

Rock's hands were overlapping her eyes. She groaned. "He got it from the party pad. There's no way he lied to Volana. He must have found it there."

By this point, Dime was almost used to doubting every truth she'd ever known, but maybe Rock was the one now being naïve.

"He did," Luja muttered. "It would have been hidden, but there's almost a code among pyrsi who use. You also develop the scent for it, something I don't have. I realized maybe he'd found some once we left. He had too much energy. Other things too. I was working up to talking to him about it." Ve winced. "He's so much older than me. I wasn't sure how. Ma-ma, please drop some of that water in your palm."

But that was tzetz. Was that Luja's plan? Her instinct was to argue. They couldn't give him *more* of the substance. Wouldn't that hurt him more? Uchitar was not responsive. His face now twitched, and his arm muscles were contracting oddly.

"Please trust me," ve stated, with a clinical tone. Vis eyes were fixed on vis hand. "There's not time."

Conflicted, Dime pulled off her gloves and opened the flask. She reached out one hand, which shook in contrast to Luja's steady one. With the other, she tipped some water into her palm.

Slowly, Luja mixed in some of the powder. Was this dangerous to touch? Should she insist on getting one of the thin trays they'd used as plates?

Forming a ball with the paste, Luja opened the fairy's mouth and reached into it, appearing to press vis fingers inside. Ve closed vis eyes, notably uncomfortable. "Go wash your hand now," ve said, and Dime realized ve was talking to her.

"Come on," Rock urged, leading her away, where Rock wet a cloth and scrubbed over and around Dime's palm.

Soon after, Luja joined them, and without words, Rock scrubbed ver as well. "Is that enough?" she asked.

"I've only got three medwipes, but I'm going to use one." After a quick trip to vis bag, ve held out a square of what looked like thick paper. Rock carefully wet it. Luja rubbed vis own hands with the sheet, then reached it out to Dime.

Whatever it contained smelled strongly, and Dime rubbed her own hands this time, trying to be thorough. But Luja had already left and was leaning over Uchitar, coaxing him to drink.

When he came back to consciousness in Luja's arms, he seemed entirely without words. His eyes flicked around, wide.

"We can't deal with it right now," ve said firmly. "We're your friends, and if you feel bad about what happened, I need you to channel it into getting going and helping us find this creep's secret weapon. Please, Uchitar. We need you. And we're not going to tell Volana; she can skip this one. I'll take care of you until we get out. I want you to trust me."

Not really knowing what to expect, Dime supposed she expected Uchitar to break into tears, or fretfully apologize as she'd seen him do before. Instead an uncomfortable grin spread across his face. His eyes continued to dart back and forth, though more slowly now. He turned slightly in vis arms, his wings adjusting.

"I need you to do what I say, for a while." Luja's voice remained firm.

He nodded.

"Right now, follow us. Let me know if you feel anything funny. Anything at all. Do you promise?"

Stumbling as they rose, ve helped him to his feet. Dime couldn't shake the image of him, curled up in pain.

As she considered it, the newts edged closer. Dime could sense their sadness, and she thought she understood that Luja asked them to keep an eye on the fairy. As ve did, Uchitar perked right back up and started striding down the path. The newts followed, and Dime realized the rest of them would have to hurry not to lose them. Still, she was glad that Rock and Luja stayed close as they pulled their gloves back on and moved ahead.

"I had to do it," Luja explained, vis eyes pleading with Dime. "He was crashing hard, and even if he survived it, we can't take him through withdrawal here. We don't have the time or supplies, nor can I see us sneaking into this weapon cave with a vomiting fairy."

That was a point of note. But not the one that mattered. "I said I would trust you, and I do." Actually, she wasn't sure if she'd said it, but anyway, she'd said it now. "How did you know how much to give him?"

"I had no idea," ve said, vis voice now shaking. "But I didn't have time to figure it out. It varies a lot, on what kind of tzetz it is and how you take it. And fairies could be different. I just hope I haven't harmed him. I assume whatever that pyr had was stronger than what Uchitar was used to, but then again since he'd already had some of that same supply, we needed to match with a strong dosage. What if I did it wrong?"

There had been such maturity and strength in Luja's words this whole time, it jarred her again to hear the vulnerability. "You did and will do everything you could." It didn't feel like enough to say. "Our minds are so complex, aren't they?"

"I wonder how valence affects them," Rock mused.

Dime wasn't sure what she meant. "Why? What?"

"Our minds. Like, with fairies. Their energies reach outward; does that leave less for self? Or solies, does reaching into ourselves drain us?"

Dime knew both fairies and solies now who felt drained or who struggled. "I don't know," was the best she could come up with.

Rock said, "I wish we talked about this. I wish it wasn't all a secret. I think we've all been using it, you know. Ella, I think she used valence to connect with the newts."

"She did," Luja murmured.

"And I think . . . I think I've used it," Rock continued. "To . . . get through things. I didn't know that's what it was, but that time . . . in the caves . . . I reached into something not fully unfamiliar. And you. I am saying all of this wrong."

"I think—" Luja now stumbled through vis words as much as Rock did. "I think that you are saying that our thoughts are not unrelated to our connection. Inner valence. Outer valence. Emotional valence. Are they all so different? They all connect to . . . like a fabric, right? The fabric of Ada-ji? Or maybe something more?"

Dime considered what they were trying to say, but her own mind was twisting now, and she was still shaken from all that had just happened. Uchitar plodded ahead, the newts marching like guards beside him.

"I don't know what to add." She paused. And said the only thing that came to mind. "I'm glad to have each of you in my life. Whatever we're all dealing with, we'll work on it together."

"I admit, D," Rock said, energy returning to her voice. "This excursion isn't my favorite thing you've had us do—and that includes flying with that stick—but we can find a way through." She hesitated.

"And when we do," Luja finished, "we'll still have each other."

Dime resolved, on those days when the steps were harder to take, that she'd remember the pyrsi who loved her. More importantly, the pyrsi whom she loved. And, she knew, that would make it better.

They'd all continued to glance up at Uchitar and the newts ahead. She was glad for the conversation.

"How is Ella?" Rock asked. "Do you know if she made it back to Sol's Reach?"

"She did." Dime wondered what their friend was doing right now. "Sounds like she walked to the Crossing and got some old connections to give her a ride home. From there, she sent us to a place I can't tell you about now, but I promise I will when I can. Dayn may still be there." A pang pricked her, like a thorn. "Then I saw her again, with Volana and Ador, and that was right before our trip to find Uchitar and you."

Dime didn't know if she should have said that. After all, they'd found Uchitar first. Should they have split up, instead? Rock had been miserable there, held by Jaza.

"Stop it," Rock murmured.

Luja pretended not to hear.

"Anyway," Dime continued, "I'll be eager to visit her when we can. She'd spent a lot of time alone in that tower, and now so suddenly, for so many new events to pile on . . . I'm glad, though. I'm glad she doesn't know where we are now."

"You mean that she'd worry? Or something more specific?" Rock heaved over a large step. Dime and Luja followed, Rock offering them each an arm in turn.

"Just the worry. I've caused her enough of that." Then, she recalled, she hadn't brought Ella into this. Ella had found *her*, gone searching for her right from the beginning, when she'd been stranded—naked and injured and being cared for by the newts. Where would she be now, without Ella? Without any of her friends?

"Let me see how he's doing." Dime sped up, to where Uchitar and the newts were moving along. "Hey. Uchitar, how are you doing?"

"I'm great!" he said, as though nothing had happened.

"I just want to thank you for being my friend," she said. If she was going to have a moment, everyone should be in.

"Ok," he replied, not looking back.

"Juni, Stern Eyes, I just want to say thank you for being my friends."

Juni made a gurgling noise, and pulled Dime up into her arms, carrying her like a basket of berries in season.

And hey, Dime just rode along there for a while, not worrying about it, until they stopped at another rockfall. Juni howled as she set

Dime down, Dime throwing her feet underneath so her boots caught the floor. She tapped her boots. "On these, Juni, remember."

Wistful, Juni slung Dime up again, much to Dime's shock. But when she realized what the feathered newt was trying to do, she obliged, showing her how to set her down, boots first, rather than on her rear.

"This way," Dime said, pulled by the diamonds. Stern Eyes stroked Juni's back, and Juni calmed a bit, as they continued on.

The passages had stayed relatively the same, more like passageways than caverns, since they'd first seen the patterns in the wall. Just from the distance they'd traveled, though, they had to be getting closer to the complex. Dime used little threads of valence to reach out and try to find it. "Oh, we're below it," she said in shock, immediately lowering her voice. "That's what felt so funny. We've passed the Great Cliff. The complex is above us now."

"Like, right up there, some Seats worker is determining how many orangecob everyone gets?" Rock said.

"Something like that."

"Can they feel the drilling?" Luja asked.

"I'm not sure," Dime said. "Here, reverberations are passing through like an instrument, and up there, it's a highly fortified structure. If they can . . . " They had to stay focused. Destroy the weapon. Then deal with the rest.

Uchitar coughed, and Dime looked over in worry. He'd calmed from his initial bursts of energy, and despite his quiet, he'd been moving along well enough. Luja said it would last like this, for a while.

"I'm sure there's a reason," Dime whispered to Luja, dropping back from the others' hearing, "but if you can help me work through it? Why couldn't he just continue to take the tzetz to avoid withdrawal? It seems that he functions better after he's had some. I'm sorry if that's an awful question. I don't *want* him to take it; I know that's a terrible thought. My point is, if he wanted to hide his use from others, he could just keep taking it."

"No, not awful. Not between us. It does seem like that now, I suppose."

Dime remembered the severity with which Uchitar had tumbled down. He must have bruises.

"There's only so much a pyr can take, though. He could have some more, then some more, and then his body will start rejecting it, and he'll start reacting again, and there won't be much you can do. So that's what happens to most pyrsi. They take what they can, then eventually they have to go through the stages again. But by that point, they are so miserable and so ashamed, they find any way to get back to that previous state of elation. It's . . . just awful."

It was.

Knowing they weren't far from the diamond caves, Dime asked the group to let her concentrate. She again sent out threads of valence, trying to feel the space around them. Now that the diamonds were close, the rock and soil and air all attached to her, like a friend.

Soon the breaks in the stone passageways grew taller and even more separated. At one steep descent, Dime worried it was too unsafe to continue. She'd already been trying not to think about what would happen if there were an additional collapse, but could they really find a path through? Understanding now, that these passages ran *under* the complex, she shuddered. These pyrsi, working away here, not understanding the danger they sat within, with the weapons of both governments so close.

Yes, she supposed, the drills were weapons. If they were being used that way. And not of governments, she reminded herself. Of pyrsi hiding behind those governments.

"We need to find a way upward," she whispered.

Juni whined. They'd both been so strong, but even Stern Eyes was faltering. Dime noticed that the two newts often walked close to each other, intertwining an arm when the space allowed it.

"Here, I think," Dime said, staring at what looked like a steep cliff, but had a strong pull upward. She could sense a flat space at the top that she could feel continued on. "I think if we climb up there, we could emerge into the top levels. Into the diamond caves themselves." She could feel them, so close.

The newts, either making the same conclusion or sensing her intent, deftly stuck their talons into the rock, easily scaling to the plateau above. Since they didn't wear glowstones, Dime could no longer see them.

Luja followed next, with Rock close behind ver. Dime motioned Uchitar forward; there was enough room for him to flap his wings almost to the top, then Rock lent him a strong arm from there.

The group had become used to Dime going last. The fact was, she had the diamond, it was tuned to her, and while she wanted to avoid noticeable valence—anything other than a sensing of the area or a faint glowstone charge—at all costs this close to the caves, she could use it if she needed to. She was sure the others had thought it.

"Be careful," Rock called down. "I agree we're getting close but there is a lot of damage here—I think this used to be a long staircase, which is maybe why it was more vulnerable to fall apart."

Dime could see upward now; the glowstones lit their faint silhouettes. Luja had moved over toward the edge. "Get back from the edge, Lu," she threw out, and using her own light to carefully look for handholds, she lifted a foot.

Uchitar moaned, and Juni jumped, getting close to Luja. Rock and Dime, above and below, both froze in place, not wanting to startle her further and knowing how steep the drop-off was right beside them, back to the level where Dime still was.

Stern Eyes lunged and grabbed Juni's arm to pull her back. Juni screamed as Stern Eyes began to lose her balance, sliding on the gravel. Luja reached over to help, spinning to propel them to better safety by the wall. Rock reached her arms out futilely, while Uchitar doubled over beside her.

"Careful," Dime called up, the word meaning nothing. She wanted to guide them but didn't know how; she couldn't see their feet or who was exactly doing what. In slow motion, two newts went flying toward Rock, near the wall, as Luja toppled backward over the edge.

Ve threw verself forward with great strength, smacking vis gloves against the rough ledge but not getting a hold. As ve fell away from Dime's sight, she created a wind and lifted it under where she thought ve was, hoping she could slow vis fall. A burst of hope surrounded them, like the heat of a fire.

A thunder exploded, of chunks of stone falling and clattering over each other to her side. She grasped at the stone before her, remembering her own accident after the escape. The rift that she'd made, and the screaming pyr. A warmth filled her. She would stay. She would face it. The divisions would not take her. Their feet, their wheels, their paws—they would all find steady ground.

They would get there together.

Feeling calmer than she should, Dime hopped down from where she'd started climbing and worked her way over, tromping over ragged stones to where she could faintly hear the sound of labored breathing behind a stonefall.

"I'm fine," Luja said, vis voice muffled. Dime still couldn't see ver, only a pile of rock. "I . . . had to use valence though. And Stern Eyes did too. She did something to me as I fell."

"I used mine too." Forget the stonefall. All three forms of valence at once, in that strength? If Neimano were near, they'd just lit a beacon. "Why were you over there?" She didn't want to scold ver, but Luja knew better than that and so there had to be a reason. Didn't there?

"I sensed something. Down, not up. I just wanted to try and sense it better. See if I could hear anything. I didn't know Juni would get spooked. She's normally not like that."

"She's tired and worried. Uchitar made a noise that scared her. Anyway. It's fine. I think we're all fine."

She leaned back and peered up from the narrow space remaining on this side of the stonefall. On the ledge above, she could only see one silhouette, which she recognized. "We're out of time, Rock." Her words echoed up the face of the stone.

"Oh, I felt it."

"Issue is Lu thinks there's something down here. Second issue is I don't see ver; whatever space ve's in was closed off. I can handle it down here, but we have to get out of this stairwell room before more of it crumbles. You find a stable place; I'll use valence to get Lu and myself out—we might as well now—and I'll meet you back up there.

"We'll all help. We're not leaving either of you."

"You can't come down here. It's too narrow and feels really unstable. Just get everyone away from the ledge. I mean. Get them back into one of the regular passages. I felt passages that way. I'll find you." She paused. "What do you think?"

A breath passed. "Ok. Hurry, though."

"Go," she said. "Check on Uchitar."

"Sol, D, I know." Rock's voice softened as they moved away, hopefully to somewhere safe.

She faced the rubble, focused on her child. The rest could wait. "Lu—can I move the stones between us?"

"You can, but let me get back a bit. Ok, move them and stop if I say 'stop'."

Dime cast the wall in light and began guiding the stones around her. At first, one at a time and when she didn't hear anything else falling, she moved more quickly, guiding several stones together, and finally just tossing them behind her into a pile.

"Do you feel that?" Dime sensed something above. Not just the boring. Something else.

"It's fairy valence," ve answered. "Someone is straining to use a lot of it. Must be Uchitar. Maybe he's doing something to distract or make a path."

Hopefully it was just that. Dime moved, faster now. Soon, she'd carved a pyr-sized opening, enough to squeeze through.

Almost. As her large backpack snagged against the edges of the stone, she jolted in place. Muttering, she stepped back and cleared a few more.

Working her way through this time, she saw that the combination of debris and whatever had been there before angled downward. At the bottom where it leveled out, she could see the glow of Luja's light.

She couldn't run. She had to be careful. But, breathing quickly, when she got there, she reached out. "You're alright?"

"I'm fine. For being at the bottom of a pit surrounded by cliffs."

This was too Dime of an answer. Rock had a point.

But there was no time to chat. "What did you sense down here? Do you still sense it?"

"I do. It's . . . dark. I just—"

What wasn't ve saying? "The room? You think the room is through here?"

"I don't want to lead us the wrong way. But something this direction is making me feel . . . bad."

Just then, the boring rumbled again. It felt more substantial now; surely they felt it in the complex. It rumbled again, and Dime leapt to shield Luja, as a spray of rock burst out from above where Rock and the others had just been.

Remembering, Dime flung out a dome of valence around them. The debris bounced away and the narrow space calmed. Dropping the barrier, she saw the area she'd just worked through was blocked again. Dime didn't like leaving them trapped, but she worried about lifting too much, about disrupting something else in the toppling structure.

She could try and make it back to the top. She could run forward. She could roll her dice. She was going to trust her child.

"Let's go," she said, holding Luja's hand as they picked their way forward, Dime deflecting lone crumbles of stone as they went. Sure enough, barely making it through a jagged crack, they emerged into clear signs of a defined passage. Not the rougher passages they'd been going through, but finely-chiseled walls with traces of vertically-stacked symbols Dime didn't recognize. Nooks and ledges, like sitting spaces.

"I think they're ok," Luja said. "It was stable ahead up there as well; I think they got out of it."

Dime squeezed vis arm reassuringly.

"We're the ones who dove into the rubble." Luja let a wavering sigh.

In a place she should have felt only despair, something yet lingered. Something that called to her . . . like . . . hope. And in the elation of still being alive, and of having a child who cared about vis friends, and thinking of Sol's light, and the night's glow and Dayn's smile, for some reason this is what popped out. "Technically *you* did, Buttons."

Ve looked back with an open mouth, then grinned. "I kept hearing that story about falling off a cliff and I heard it was a life-affirming experience. You're *right*, Ma-ma. I feel great. Now, let's go show Third Seat Neimano what we think of his weapon."

Interlude

The interviewer leaned back against her chair, tapping the open folder. "I see your coursework is spelled out, but your recommendations are a little light."

Harm it. Orna had known it would come to this. He tried to hold the smile on his face. "My primary instructor wrote a whole page, discussing the value of my contributions."

"I saw it," she said, running a finger across her chin as she looked up, her gaze landing on his tattoos. "I'm a little more curious about your background. We pride ourselves on our culture at this office."

A bird squawked outside the window. *Oh, I know.*

Orna felt himself slipping. He couldn't let himself slip. His deskmate from school, Aloc, and vis spouse—he couldn't remember the ji'pyr's name—they'd both warned him the pyrsi here were soft Pillarites. He'd hoped it wasn't true. It was exactly the kind of work he wanted, and he knew it paid well. Maybe he could get his own home. Rent a toothcar to visit his family. Prola must have grown so much by now.

He tried to keep his voice level. "My background is well-detailed in the application, including examples of my work and recommendations from the teams on which I studied. I'd love to discuss it and talk about the work I could do here."

"Where did you grow up?" she asked, reaching to pour more tea.

With my family, he almost answered. He couldn't. Righteousness wouldn't get him a job. It wouldn't break the holds these pyrsi had on power in this city. Not that he wasn't a little righteous. One of his friends had suggested he forge a record. There were high-class homegroups in the mountains that kept so private, no one would go check his claim.

"No," he'd said. He wasn't going to live a lie. He was proud of who he was.

Orna took a breath. "Burge, perhaps we can chat about family over a drink sometime—I'm very proud of mine. For now, I'd like to draw your attention to the file I put together. I believe I've shown a lot of promise and know I could learn so much from working at a respected institution such as this one."

"Thank you," she said. "I agree." She flipped the file over. "Good, we have your address. I'll contact you if we decide to move forward. It's been my pleasure," she added, standing.

He wanted to argue it. He wanted to ask on what basis she had to assume he wouldn't do well based on the location of his family or the fact they'd lived off of the orchard, on a hillside so beautiful he doubted she could imagine it. He wanted to say that yeah, he wished he had a better instructor too, but the clerk making placements had noticed his wrist chain, a symbol of growth and accomplishment that was a long-standing tradition in his village. And so he'd been placed with that pyr. He'd still done his best.

Glancing down to the expensive used suit he'd found just for this event, he noted how the ruffled sleeve covered his wrist chain. He pushed the sleeve back, making sure the chain was exposed as he rose from the chair, letting it jingle as he turned.

He held his head high as he walked back out into the hallway.

"You just need pyrsi that are going to fit in," he heard her saying to the clerk in the background.

As he walked back onto the crowded sidewalk, he nearly snarled at the pyr in the Sol's Pillars vest who'd just stepped up from the street. The pyr didn't seem to pay him mind, but did look over at whatever sound Orna had made.

"You don't have to be so angry," xe said, shaking xyr head as the pyr stepped past into the building.

Act 3

COLLAPSE

Muffled cracks and groans reverberated through the underground structures and, as they drew closer to the diamonds, she could hear them ringing in fear. Perhaps it was strange to say that diamonds feared their own destruction, but there was a life in the caves that knew the Violence in its core. Her own pendant trembled against her chest.

Without the urgency caused by their simultaneous blast of valence, Dime would have stopped to study the area they now navigated. With carved columns and unfamiliar designs, it would be like opening a book she had never before seen, and she longed to stay and absorb its quiet truth. There must be layers of old story here in Ada-ji's center. Yet all she'd ever been offered was a caution that though Sol's pyrsi won the Great War, it—or the Violence—must never return.

This aggravated her. All pyrsi had the right to know about the world they traveled, their own failures as well as their triumphs. They should study it. Like the history of a pyr, there should be a similar concept: history of all pyrsi. A subject in school, even, like numbers or health.

Luja's eyes were also drawn to the old symbols. "There is so much we don't know," ve said in a low tone. Dime nodded, though ve probably couldn't see her own wistful glances as they hurried forward.

The passage curved suddenly, without the nuanced shape of the larger section. Crumbled piles narrowed the way, and Dime edged over to a stone wall, one that pulled her, though with a dark unease.

Stopping there and removing her gloves, Dime pressed against the cool stone, her ear also but that was more symbolic as she wasn't sure what it was she was hoping to find. "It's here," she said, twitching at the tingle in her bare palms. "Through here. There is an extraordinary concentration of diamonds on the other side, and something else, too. A field of valence. Old valence."

It was frustrating that she was so very new to the secrets of the world, when she'd lived so long above them. She had no idea what any of it meant. What this place was. How diamonds could radiate so much fear when they served only to amplify.

Her senses told her the force beyond was old valence. But what did that mean? She didn't feel anyone actively casting; it felt more like something built and left behind. She wasn't sure if it was the way a glowstone could stay alight, requiring occasional attention, or more like the way a thin screen could gather sediment and become thick. Maybe both. Perhaps like the golden barrier she'd made in Sol's Reach, outside the den: she supposed had she left it in place, fortified it over time, built in elements of repeat—it was like that. Except the intent felt ill, she realized, like the door Neimano had made to block the entrance. She shuddered.

A barrier to protect and a barrier to exclude were not the same thing. Their very fiber, she now understood, was made of different thread. Different valence.

Luja expressed no such confusion over the ideas of fields or old valence, so she didn't bother to convey all of this to ver.

"So that's what you felt back there," she said instead. "By coming in this way, we cut right to the lower reaches of the caverns. It's in here." She tapped the stone. "Like we're on the outside of a room."

"How do we get inside?"

That was the question. She wondered if the others above could reach this place, or if the way from the upper passages had been blocked. Perhaps the group had found the open path, and were the only ones that could get through, and Dime and Luja were stuck at a dead end, beside the room in some ancient cellar. And what they sought was right through that wall.

Her chest fluttered in panic. No. She had to focus on getting into the room. Starting here. Backtracking was an option, but one that would cost valuable time.

Certainly Luja knew that with both of their valence and Dime's own pendant, they could break through the layers of rock and valence by force. But at what cost? What would be the risk? They weren't going to do anything that could risk the safety of the complex above. And what would be the effect to the valence field inside?

Neimano had to have a way in; they needed to find it. Fast.

The passage curved back and away. Taking it would place them farther from the room. She'd rather stay close. Instead of lighting the whole area, she generated a single ball of light and swung it around like a lantern. The shadows caught a small collapse, above, a little opening atop a pile of stones. She closed her eyes and reached upward. It was not only a pocket; it led somewhere.

Since Neimano knew they were close, Dime no longer worried about using her abilities. "Hold your bag out front," she said, swinging her own around. Luja imitated her, grasping vis bag tightly, and Dime pointed up. She lifted both bags, guiding Luja's first toward the opening. Ve crouched and placed vis feet onto the rough ledge, eking out a tiny sound as vis feet scrabbled against the gravel. Ve pushed forward into the jagged space. Turning, ve extended a hand to help guide Dime in, and Dime released her control of the bags. Once they were both steady, Dime brought the ball of light closer and dimmed it.

They scooched through the opening and hopped down into a passage, with plenty of room to stand. They put their bags back on and hurried along. Dime's own sense of urgency was pinching in her chest, and by Luja's pace, ve felt it too.

There were several smaller interweaving passages here, many curving upward. The layout felt unnecessarily complex, and in the darkness Dime wondered what this place had once been. Without speaking, they motioned to each other, indicating whatever elements of the caves and of the valence that they sensed. Each time the passage changed shape, the silence did as well, the slow flow of air changing pitch and the echoes of their breath with it. Like a game of hide-and-seek but with an unknown partner, they considered the options, and searched any places that might provide a way in, eliminating those that did not.

After turning back twice, and then again to where she felt the strongest pull, they were left with one option: *nothing*. Both stopped in place.

It only looked like nothing; Dime knew this junction they had reached was distorted with valence. Perhaps the opposite of a glow stone, similar to what Agent X had done in xyr room, the light had been removed from the stone face. Not just to say that it was dark, or even like the encompassing darkness of the caves where they'd slept. More—it was a virtual nothingness that they faced, screaming danger in its silence. Dime blinked out the ball of light; it did no good here.

"It's ok," she comforted, knowing that any pyr who faced such a thing would feel fear, but especially one as filled with light as Luja was. Ignoring her eyes, she used valence to sense her way into the void. "Don't move," she hastily added. "The floor ends, and the door is more than a jump past it. The dropoff can't be too deep; we were just down there, but there's a stream of valence flowing through, woven with the barrier."

"A moat," Luja said.

"Like in realms? Yes, I suppose so." She felt deeper into the space. "It's designed for fairies, requiring both fairy valence and also wings."

"I think a soly could get in," Luja murmured. "But Neimano might not know that."

There wasn't time to debate it.

Dime sensed the knobless door and found it nothing like the other such doors inside the complex, like the one at the end of Ferala's secret passage. This door did not want to be opened. Drawing more valence than she was used to, she slowly dragged the stone slab from its place. Sweat blossomed on her back. The stone groaned open and angled back against its huge hinges. She didn't waste her energy on lighting the stones inside, for the valence was still there. Without her eyes, then. She would find a way.

The old valence worried her, but the entrance felt passable, as if opening the door had rerouted it.

"I'm not staying here," Luja whispered.

Ve wouldn't be safe either way, and so Dime deferred to vis judgment. They swung their bags again in front, and Dime lifted them. She and her child clung to them in the darkness and floated across, avoiding the flow of valence and gliding into the unseeable space.

Each holding the other's arm, they stepped together onto the ledge.

The shock hit them as quickly. It did not hurt, and it passed through in an instant. A spray of green light stayed, illuminating a tall, diamond-walled chamber that extended below them, with spiral steps winding down.

She let go of Luja and curled her fingers in and out. They put their bags back on and exchanged glances in the eerie glow. Then, the valence had been an alarm. Still, this terrified her. Walking right into his valence, what if *it* had been the weapon? She'd never considered such an idea until the shock passed through her. They were alive. They could move. She breathed in.

Dime did not try and light the room further; she wanted to touch as little as she could until they could find what rested here, destroy it, and leave. Green light streamed out from the rounded wall, flickering now and illuminating the room in harsh bursts. The air smelled metallic. This room—or wherever they were. Was this it? Could it be Neimano's secret . . . whatever?

If Neimano wanted to have a special basement to store his weapon, she wasn't going to glorify it with fancy names.

Luja gasped and gripped Dime's arm, and Dime remembered ve had never seen a diamond wall before. Dime had never seen one like *this*. There could be no greater concentration of the clear crystals in all of Ada-ji. Of that, she was certain.

Of course Neimano would choose this place.

These walls had not been left to nature. In the oddly shaped space, the light patterns through the dense, smoothly faceted diamond crystals fought the greenness of the valence, seeking to shine in rainbows. What resulted was an impossibility: a profoundly unstable battle.

Tall pillars carved with the same symbols they'd just seen rose around the sides. The staircase they stood on grew narrower as it unfurled downward, almost disappearing behind one of the columns.

At the bottom was a raised platform of stone, formed into a rounded table in its center. If the table had been etched at some point, it was barely detectable now, with an imperfect surface that only whispered its past. Two chairs rested on one side, worn, broken perhaps, as they leaned crookedly against the chattering diamonds. She couldn't tell if they were furnishings of Neimano's era or not, but they hadn't been used in ages either way.

On the table, surrounded by tall, padded stands, nested ten grimy vials, each sealed with a bulb of undyed wax and carrying a thick layer of dust. A shiver crept through Dime's body and she struggled to maintain her composure. Her thoughts were mostly with her child, but she also knew that whatever happened, she could not leave these vials intact.

Her arm twitched, or maybe it was her old wing muscles. Was this really the curse, preserved these twenty-plus cycles? Who had that substance killed? Her original family, maybe? That idea was as dark as the void outside this space. As unnatural as the light inside.

How would she destroy them? Hopefully she could use valence to destroy them without touch, but she was nervous also, about fumes. Maybe she could create a barrier, pour the liquid through a crack and crush the glass—she still had some water—but none of this with Luja in reach.

"Stay here," Dime directed, as she took a cautious step downward and forced her mind to stay alert. "Remember we don't know exactly how it spreads, but you can't get close. Stay here until I can destroy it." She wished now that she had left Luja outside, an idea that had pained her just strides ago. But now, looking down at Neimano's sick treasure and fighting the fog of her own horror, she wished that Luja were anywhere but inside this room. There wasn't time, now that they'd passed the field of valence. They must act.

"Stop!" Luja shouted, brushing Dime's back. "Stop! Please!" Vis voice lowered. "What do you think that is?"

Sensitive to the narrow, twisting staircase, Dime turned. She didn't have time now for the Aoch's doubts, yet she stopped. Hadn't Luja heard the discussion? She'd told ver, right?

"The curse. To use as a weapon. Now, let me destroy it. We don't have time."

"I know! Ma-ma, it's not the curse." Ve ran vis hand over vis forehead and back over vis scalp. "Tell me again? What was Project Diamondsong? *Please*," ve implored.

She didn't like to talk about it. But she couldn't remember how much she'd told Luja and there wasn't time to parse it. She hoped to Sol Luja wasn't taking the last moments they'd need, and she answered as succinctly as she could, having to reach into an ugly cabinet in her mind just to shake out the details.

"Lots of pyrsi died of a disease. They called it the curse. It was contagious and vile. The Fo-ror blamed the Ja-lal; I'm not aware of evidence that supports that. Neimano found ten sick ba'pyrsi from low class families and removed their wings. He planted them in places of power within Lodon. He—"

"The ba'pyrsi all had this curse?"

Isn't that what Ferala had said? Yes, she thought so. "Yes. He did that so no one would miss them. They were ba'pyrsi that he could just record had died, and no one would question it."

"But you didn't."

Didn't what? Oh. Right. She wasn't dead. Though they couldn't continue to stand here—

"You're naturally immune. This isn't the curse." Luja was tapping vis head, a little roughly, and Dime tried to think what ve was saying. "He chose you because you had the curse and you survived it. I've never heard of a disease that could hold its form outside of a body for too long, definitely not for two epochs. If you would have told me— Anyway, it doesn't matter. You can't touch it."

"You said I was immune."

"You're carrying the curse."

Dime stood, frozen.

"Ma-ma, I'm sorry. It's what makes sense. Harm, he probably injected you with more of it. Ba'pyrsi's bodies are so . . . Oh, harm. Harm. It fits. That's where he kept it. *You.*"

"Then what the kill is that?" She pointed helplessly down at the wickedly brooding table. Ten vials. "Ten!"

"I know. You're right. That's part of what I'm thinking. A duller, is what I can figure. They're used when pyrsi have allergic reactions; they slow the body's response to interference. You take someone's blood who's affected and tune a dulling substance. Medics, we decide when they're safe to use. And maybe he tested it." Luja took a breath. "As long as the body is actively countering it when the sample is taken, you can make some. If they did it right, it could revive the effects in you for a short while; allow you to transfer it to others before your body returned to immunity." Vis voice lowered. "So much effort to refine and store it in such a short time. And the *risks* of not *telling* you."

"Can a dormant disease kill you?" Dime felt disconnected, like her tether to the events of the last bells had been yanked from her with no warning. But they were in a hurry, she was able to remember. She needed to get down there and destroy it. There was no losing her concentration this time, not like in the past. She had to focus.

"Yes, they can be toxic. Depends on the disease. Depends on the pyr. Xyr body. Xyr activities. The concentration. The treatment. Immunity slips. Other victims are dead?"

Dime nodded. "Four dead. One missing. One . . . no, two . . . harmed. At least two."

"Could be several things. Could be the toxicity. I'm *sure* he injected you with more. A ba'pyrsi's body—no, sorry, no time. Could be trauma related to the unresolved valence. Ma-ma. Listen to me. Leave and shut the door. Right now."

"I'm not going to leave you—"

"I promise I'll come back. I promise. We can talk about the rest of it later. I'm a medic. I know what I'm talking about. Do you want to stand here and let Neimano find and kill us, or do you want to trust me?"

"He was willing to spread the curse."

"Please leave. I promise I'll do my best to stay safe. I can handle it. Ma-ma. We signaled him. We can't just stay here. *Go.*"

"What if you're wrong?"

Luja threw vis arms up.

Sol.

Dime staggered up the top couple stairs as she flew back to the lightless corridor. Using no effort at all now, for how much her own diamond was interacting with those around her, she pushed the heavy panel closed, ready to help open it again if ve didn't soon emerge.

Her thoughts flipped between protection for her child and the idea of what she really was.

Am I too dangerous to exist? I came here saying I would destroy the curse. If I'm the curse . . . Dime didn't know how to continue. Was her existence too much of a risk? How could she have let Luja stay there? If weapons should all be destroyed, what should happen to her?

She stood at the edge of the darkness, a pit before her. And she stood, scared, waiting, hoping that she was not harming her child as she stood here, helpless, confused—scared.

Each passing stride grew her panic as much as it numbed her, and for all that she'd escaped, and ran, and ran back, and confronted, and learned, now she just stood here. Waiting. Her fate in the hands of her child. Her child's fate in hers. She couldn't leave without ver. She wouldn't. If something went wrong? Should she go into the room and check? Luja said wait. She waited.

It had been too long. She needed to go in.

The door grated open. She sensed ver but could not see. A form, hovering in the open doorway. "Ma-ma," ve wheezed. "I'm ready."

"Hold tight," she called, and with every piece of her, she sensed Luja as she guided ver over. Dime would have embraced ver. But Dime was tainted. Dime was dangerous. She was the weapon.

"Stop it!" Luja hissed. Then, quieter, "You've gone this long. You can't think like that. Neimano is the weapon. Not you. Think how long you've interacted with us, embraced us, been part of our lives. The others, too. There's no evidence of spread. We don't even know if it would have worked! Please, Ma-ma, when I get back, I'll study you. I'll work it. We've expelled other disease remnants. The medics of Lodon would love to work this. Please. Your body is different but let me try." Luja stopped, out of breath. "If we find a way, we'll pass it to any fairies who survived. We'll end it forever."

Dime still stood, a corpse hovering in a world to which she could not return. "I was meant to live," she breathed out. "But only to betray or kill others. One. Or the other." She wavered in place.

"Not meant. Not meant." Luja squeezed her arm. "The vials. They're gone. We have to go," ve said.

"Are you ok?" Dime whispered. "Did they—"

"I'll be well. Don't worry. We have to go. I'm sorry. Just . . . stop worrying for right now and put your trust in me a while longer. I'll never let go."

As if reading the collapse of Dime's thoughts, Luja pulled her by the arm, pulled her from the lightless precipice, and down the corridor.

Whatever had been done by the drills had reached a new force, now. Or perhaps it was Neimano, barreling toward them. Or whatever Luja had done to destroy the vials. Or the green energy that they'd broken.

A spray of stone pummeled them as they stumbled down the passage, Luja's strong hand gripped tight to her own. "This way," ve called. "Now, here." Dime felt her bag being pushed back in front. "Take us up there." Together, they flew as Dime, somewhere else, numbly moved them in the direction of Luja's prompting. "Now this way."

"D! Sol, D!" A familiar voice, though raspy and strained, greeted her.

"She's not well. We need to leave." Luja was the one who spoke.

"He's not either." The first voice. Dime felt herself swept up into warm, feathery arms as a scream surrounded her.

"They're all leading away. I can't find anything."

"It's ok. We got there. We found the room. We destroyed it. But we have to go. The way we came?"

"No, it's blocked. This way to the main entrance—we've been there before. He'll know anyway, and your mother can get us through it. Go, go."

A groan issued beside her, and she saw Uchitar bouncing along, as if floating. No, dark feathers surrounded him. Were they both being carted by newts? The newts lurched, pushing everyone to the side.

Streaks of fire burned past and warmed her face, and Dime, unwanted in any land, wondered if this was the end.

It could not be the end. Her child was here. Her friends. Dayn and Tum; what would they think if she never returned?

"Ma-ma!" Luja screamed.

Dime leapt down from Juni's arms, and around them her barrier burst again, illuminating the whole group in golden, sparkling light. Neimano, who she now saw stumbling toward them, hurled more fire their way, but it crackled and singed against the golden sphere. Rock cried out, behind her.

"What have you done?" His thin voice snarled at them.

Neimano was here. Neimano had thrown fire at them. At Juni. At Rock. At her *child*. Not air this time, *fire*.

In addition to his stilted movements, Neimano's appearance surprised her. His normally styled hair was pulled haphazardly together, and his robes were singed and torn. She was so tired of this pyr. So tired of his interference and cruelty. In a world filled with love, this one pyr had done such harm. Toppled so many game-planks of division, mistrust. Greed. While others had allowed him to keep power.

Uchitar, imprisoned for his troubles while a pyr like this set the rules that put him there. An abomination.

"It's too late," she said between breaths. "They're all gone now. I assume you've unblocked the path; we're going through."

"Did you . . . did you open them?"

Dime understood. That's why he'd acted to kill; why he'd finally crossed that line. His own gross weapon, the cause. He worried she was infected right now, blossoming with the serum and reinvigo-rating the curse, the one that was meant for the towers of Lodon. While his worry was not her priority, what he might do was.

"They are destroyed," she said. "We are leaving, and you should too. It's not safe here."

Neimano blasted the golden field around them with fury and malice and—she could feel it—desperation. Air, fire, the smallness of his self. It didn't matter. The corridor was wide enough to pass; Dime held her friends close, moved the barrier with them as they ran forward, and led them toward Neimano's invisible door. They moved quickly now, and Neimano struggled to keep up. As they disappeared from his view, she dropped the barrier, folding forward and breathing heavily. Luja peered down with concern.

New reverberations intensified around them; surely the complex wasn't safe. She hoped the other Seats had focused on saving the pyrsi within it, rather than chase after absurd schemes and the tiny flight of this pyr.

The heart of Ada-ji would collapse any moment now. All of it. The chambers of the Seats, the offices, the diamond caves. Whether she had done it, or Neimano, or the drills, or Luja, or something new, she didn't know. But it was inevitable, like the cry of a mountain avalanche. And Dime knew, in overwhelming situations, there was a time to escape. To save hope. Preserve it, so that it could bloom.

Both doors loomed ahead. First, the physical door that Dime easily swung open with valence. Then, Neimano's valence door, not quite left open, but not as secured as when it had been closed. She flung her hand upward and thrust will into the boundary. Chartreuse sparks erupted, clearing them a path.

Dime stopped, urging the group forward.

First, Stern Eyes, carrying Uchitar. Then Luja, Juni, and Rock. Rock shook her head in cold fervor and trust, and Dime nodded, obeying her silent command.

Voices echoed down the corridors—some system of valence like what they had used at commons, but now issuing a repeated command in a deep, cold voice. Not Neimano's, but likely one of his High Guards.

"Arrest. Arrest. There is an urgent order for the arrest of Diamond the Traitor. The wingless Fo-ror is here, in the complex, causing the distress that you feel. By the order of the Seats. By the order of Sha. Capture the Traitor. Do not let her escape."

Dime hesitated. "I agreed to ask Layanie before going through."

"Harm, D, the arrest negates that! And the fact that he's trying to kill us!"

"Seat Layanie is kind," Uchitar choked out. "Ve will understand."

They grasped each other as the ground shook, not just distant rumbles, but a deep shudder. An angry groan.

Wingless Fo-ror.

Whatever happened in her life, Dime decided this wasn't a place she needed to come back to. And never would.

But harm if she was going to let it be destroyed.

"Everyone. Go. Please."

She expected an argument, but Rock and Luja held hands, and with the others ahead of them, they all ran. Neimano had been slowed, but surely he was on his way. She couldn't worry about that yet.

Only when she saw her friends move, saw the back of her child growing smaller in the distance, did she squeeze her diamond, letting it press into the fibers of her hand. She did not care what she used up of it, or what she had left. It was never hers. Or never should have been.

Glitter of gold and sparks of blue burst through her like an orchestra of sound, filling her. Her mind reached into every stone, every crevice, every sparkling facet. She hoped and she urged and she remembered and she hoped again, and she strained, and she hurt and she said *I will not watch you fall.*

She asked the other diamonds to join her. To untie what pyrsi had done. To dissolve the threads of ill woven through the passages, to calm the tremors of the drills. She could not affect the damage, but the strain. The fissures. She thought of Ada-ji. She thought of its shared heart. Every grain was important. Every pathway. The insects and the dust and the old and new air. She brought it all into her being, and like a lullabye she breathed.

Shh.

Shh.

We will not abandon you.

Slowly, piece by piece, the rocks settled. She felt the fairies running from the complex. The insects scuttled to shelter but did not leave. Dime protected them. Admired their stubbornness. Their connectedness. Their simplicity and their complexity.

She comforted the land, in the same awkward way that she'd tried to be a good mother. To only know how to say that she loved them. And that she cared. To try and reassure. And maybe a song of less appropriate origin, but the words were never the point.

Ada-ji was her child. Ada-ji was her parent. She calmed ver.

It was not a solution; it was only time.

Somewhere in haze and exhaustion she remembered that she had saved Neimano too. That in her calming, she gave him the ability to leave. To put pyrsi in more harm. As she had before.

It could not be her weight alone. Neimano was not her weight.

But he would, right now, be in her pursuit. Because if he worried she carried the curse, he'd realized that she was carrying it here. In his home. Not hers.

Dime returned back to the world, back to a place where her name was being called out, where lies were projected and truth concealed, where she worried for her friends, where it was never time for a break. Her hand still gripped the diamond pendant. Perhaps, she thought, its power would be drained but it was not. It rang, as if offering more. She released it, hastening to consider her options.

She could walk through the complex with an order blaring for her arrest and pyrsi in confusion and fear. Perhaps they would detain her, hold her with ropes, or worse. Sure, she could escape again. But she worried about destabilizing the situation further, or escalating the Violence. Maybe it would come to that. But she would not be the reason why. No more hiding, she'd said. If she were just in a tower, she could move to a window and fly away. Why was she in a cave? Why was she always in a cave?

Frustrated, she yearned for Sol. For shade. For open spaces.

For light.

Laughing, she considered it. Taking a page directly from High Guard Ulkanet's book, she turned off the lights as she strode through each hall. Enough to confuse. Just long enough that she could storm through, take the next turn, take out the next lights. The hallways were emptier than before, with pyrsi leaving on their own, so she hurried on. And when the daylight of the entrance came into view, voices layered and jumbled and she saw a massive crowd gathered in the sunlight, under and around the huge stone arch. Trees watched, past the large clearing.

From the shade of the passage, she pulled Batu's travel blanket from her bag.

"I'm sorry," she said, genuinely feeling the parting of the striped maroon fleece. If only she'd still had that banner. "I'm sure you'll find a good home."

Taking out a paper, she scribbled a message.

Deliver directly:

Seat Layanie – He is still here and dangerous. What he says is not true.

H.S. Ferala – Tell ver. And give us time. Drop any search. I'll be in contact soon.

Edging toward the front, she propelled the blanket up over the stone arch and away with valence, while draping it to suggest something concealed underneath. The crowd screamed and pointed, and wings flapped and launched in pursuit. The note fluttered down toward the High Guards as others flew up to catch it.

In the commotion, Dime held her bag forward and launched up with them. Flying upward, and with her white hair, she almost fit in, and no one saw her as she rose and then parted, not flying high but lowering down near the path, away from anyone's gaze.

She flew now, without any doubt where her friends were. They'd continued to leave, trusting her, and now they hid in the forest outside. And she held her bag and raced toward them, swirling in loops and in and out of trees to avoid being followed, even if anyone had noticed her in the commotion. She landed away from the group and ran, without valence. She ran and ran and her breath hurt, and when she saw strong Luja, beautiful Rock, Uchitar huddled to himself, and Juni and Stern Eyes, holding each other in vigil, only then did she collapse into the leaves and needles.

Only then did she lie on her back and look upward, and through the towering spires of the trees she saw it: Sol. Bright. Glaring. The light, shining down on her. Too bright for her eyes, and she turned away, laughing softly, under her breath, not caring if the others saw.

When, finally, she settled, she glanced around at the group. They were not well.

Uchitar's head fell between his knees. His knot of white hair fell forward, strands pulled against it as though smoothed back down by his hand.

Stern Eyes held Juni like a cub, yet the elder newt trembled. Her toes rattled against the rough ground.

Rock watched Dime, intently, as if they were playing realms and Rock had to predict Dime's moves to choose her own.

Luja paced in circles, muttering to verself, much the way Dayn did when perplexed.

"We destroyed the weapon," Dime said.

Yet, she would not lie.

"We destroyed a serum he kept. Luja did. One was made for each of his victims, a final plan if our infiltration failed. There is a reason it was a serum. I . . . have reason to believe I have the curse now. Dormant, inside me. I need you to know that. You may want to distance yourself from me, and I won't fault you."

The silence chilled her.

"I told you. He is the killer. Not you." Luja nearly spat. "You will live your life, and if it harms others then we'll adapt. We're making it . . . too complicated." Ve spun on vis boots, turning more to Rock than to Dime. "I will not be forced by anyone's righteous views. It's more complicated than that.

"I know what you're all thinking, whether you want to or not. Can my mother—my mother—exist? Or is she dangerous? Dangerous for what was done to her? Dangerous because she didn't stop Neimano? No, again and again she allowed him to escape. Do you know where these thoughts lead? Shifting the blame to a single pyr, for what everyone has done? Asking someone *else* to be a killer, even in the depths of your thoughts, is a tremendous burden. It is a horrible, horrible burden, that you don't throw on someone, especially when *you* don't have to do it."

Luja's comments were disjointed, and Dime wasn't sure why ve was yelling at Rock; if anything, Rock would be the last to leave her. Dime's fingers twitched. Ve spun back to Dime. "And stop calling it that. Don't say that word again. 'AD-1'—there, I named it. You survived AD-1." Ve sat down, vis head falling into vis hands.

"I'm not changing a Soltweaked thing," Rock said, reaching into her bag and pulling out a somehow not-squished wrap of root crisps. "Nothing has changed except what we know, and yeah, sometimes that's the worst." She crunched into a crisp. "So what do we do now?" She'd turned to Dime. "I could feel you fixing things, but the drills are still running. I think whatever you did in that room caused an issue too. And then the blasts of fire seemed to harm the whole place off. Like, Sol felt it. Sha. The whole Fo-ror power structure is now enraged and probably in chaos. The Sol's Pillars are running over Lodon, and I doubt even the Circles can look away from that for long. It's going to have to be more than just you fixing things." She wiped crisp oil from her mouth with the back of her hand.

That was the question, wasn't it. What now? Dime was tired of having to answer that over and over, like none of them were ever allowed to settle into their existence again. She'd wanted to work for change. Now that she'd seen the world, she could never look away. Just sometimes breaks would be nice too. Peace.

Everyone deserved that.

Did she mean that? Did Neimano deserve rest? Peace? A cruel pyr. She watched a chubby, multi-legged insect crawl over her foot and disappear into the leaves.

Food. Water. Rest. Care. Peace. Yes, everyone should have these and she wasn't going to let even Neimano take that belief from her.

He'd taken enough.

She paused. Perhaps Neimano could not have peace. That was his own doing, his own consequence for causing harm. A tragedy.

Juni began to whimper, leaned up against Stern Eyes, and let a long, slow whine. Dime wasn't worried about the sound; it could be a calling bird and the Fo-ror were likely unfamiliar with how newts vocalized anyway. But she was concerned for her friend.

Approaching slowly, Dime held out her arms. Stern Eyes made small puff sounds as Dime ran her hands down Juni's feathers. They were in too much danger to sing loudly, but she hummed a small song, under her breath. She knew the newts had better hearing, and music didn't need to be loud.

Juni's chattering calmed and Stern Eyes' puffs did along with them. She didn't bother to translate through Luja. Sometimes, just being there was all the communication needed.

With a sudden nervous feeling that Juni was going to pull Dime back into her lap, Dime patted her and moved into the circle with the others.

She glanced around. "How did you get out?" Dime hadn't had a chance to really consider it. "You don't exactly blend in." Forget the solies. She was picturing the reaction to two large newts racing through the office spaces. Assuming they went that way. She tried to imagine Juni in chambers.

"It was Uchitar," Luja answered, vis voice quieter now. Uchitar did not look up. "Some pyrsi were leaving anyway, because of the shaking. Others started to follow and call after us. Some stood in front but we just moved around them. As we got to the entrance, the pyrsi behind us stopped, I guess because the guards were there. Then the guards tried to follow us, and Uchitar turned to them, including the ranking ones, and shouted like a storybook hero. He was all like *Do Not Follow Us*, and the guards were so confused why this regular fairy was commanding them they started to argue, and before they could figure out what to do about it, we'd made it into the trees.

"We could see the huge crowd bursting out the front by that point, but we all ran really fast and got here, out of sight from above. At least until you caught up."

"Nice," Dime said. She thought back to her conversations with Ella about fairies not being used to the idea that orders could be disobeyed, especially not from the Seats.

"I wasn't like a hero," Uchitar said, his voice strained. "I just didn't want any of us to have to go back in there."

Perhaps being a hero could be that simple.

"I slowed everyone down, too. Almost got us caught. I'm not used to running by foot, and—"

Dime marveled at this, considering the physical state of the pyr, his not-young body slamming between tzetz highs and feelings of failure. In fact, she had a sense he'd taken one more dose. He might later regret that boldness at the gates, especially if he ever learned the details of his earlier removal from the prison. Her heart filled. Despite all his troubles, he'd done what he could to help them.

She would do everything she could to help Uchitar.

"They are out looking for us," she said, realizing that was a silly comment, as the group had been waiting here, specifically for her to catch up. "Sorry, you know that. Anyway, let's find someplace safer."

"Ask the newts," Luja said. Vis voice was growing thin. "They're great at hiding."

"Good idea," she said. "Can you translate?"

"Oh, sorry. I forget."

Dime knew what ve forgot. Now that they were outside again, Luja was used to Tum being there, taking the lead in the translation. Dime felt the same way. She was tired of her family being fragmented. They should be together. At her core, it was all she wanted and no one should keep taking that from her.

Stern Eyes drooped forward; Dime swore there were new wrinkles on her face. It was Juni who stood, offering Stern Eyes an arm to help lift her. Sniffing, the younger newt bent down and began to shuffle around, in nonsensical spirals.

Without warning, she bolted, and the others raced to gather their bags and follow. Stern Eyes split the distance, stopping a few times to ensure the pyrsi were still in sight. Fine. In sniff.

Just as they caught up to her, she'd wriggled through a nest of vines, not flinching as her scales and feathers squeezed through the mess. Their skin more sensitive, Dime almost used valence to create a pathway, then remembered that she shouldn't. "Sorry, no valence; Neimano could sense it," she explained, as Stern Eyes pushed through.

"Here," Uchitar said, crouching further down. "I think we can get through here."

He pulled a branch back with unexpected strength and waited as the others slithered through on their chests and arms. Once she got through, she glanced around. They were inside of a tangle of vines, competing for light, she supposed, and leaving a hollow space in the middle. The top was mostly covered, except for one small patch where Sol streamed brightly in at an angle, shining on a lone patch of green. Fortunately, there was enough room for the six of them and their bags without disturbing the defiant little patch, or risking being seen from above it. She turned to watch the space they'd crawled through, wondering how the larger Uchitar with his wings would make it in.

He came popping through, almost in a ball. Dime ached, knowing the way he'd suffer for the repeat usage and subsequent lack of care, but realizing that Luja was right. What mattered now was their ability to continue on, to complete their mission. But Uchitar needed help. Harm, they all needed help.

"I think we'd hear anyone nearby," Rock said, plunking down to one side. "Let's let them search. They'll assume we're still running, and meanwhile we can rest."

"I agree. Lu, Uch?"

They both nodded. Dime didn't like the way Uchitar's eyes twitched.

"I don't think we should fall asleep," she offered, "but we can still recover a bit before getting away. Maybe a bell? I'm not going back to party place, though. You can."

Rock set down her bag. "We can't just storm Volana's again."

"I know." Dime had been thinking about this. "I'll get Tum and I'm taking my children back to Sol's Reach. Find somewhere remote. I won't risk walking into a village, but Luja can. Ve can watch Tum for a while, and—"

A noise interrupted them, and both newts were on their sides, snoring. She supposed the long, guttural growls were snoring. Rock chortled, and she and Luja exchanged smiles. Even Uchitar relaxed a bit, gazing with fondness at their companions.

"Should we worry about the sound?" Luja asked.

Uchitar shook his head. "No. No one I know has any ideas what newt snores sound like. If I were in the forest and heard this, I'd assume it was a barip and stay sharp nails away."

"You have barips here too?" Dime couldn't help but ask. "They live in the mountains. All the way in the nor of Ada-ji."

"They live mostly outforest here," he answered. "But sometimes they wander in. They leave pyrsi alone and so we leave them alone. Anyway." The fairy turned around suddenly, facing away from the group.

Dime didn't know what to do. Her friend suffered, still affected by tzetz, the phases of recovery not only having been swept from him, but delayed, to relive again. How painful the concept of a relieving high would be, knowing that it only swung a pyr farther from the agony of recovery.

"I'm glad you're here," she said, trying to say something.

"How could you be?" he snapped, spinning back around. "I'm a wreck. I'm nothing, and it's all my fault. You should leave me here and go on. All I did was drag you down, and all I've done is drag Volana down too. It's time for me to go my own way. Why would you continue with someone that hurts pyrsi again and again, without hope?"

Dime paused. Rock didn't.

"That's not all true." Rock's voice was firm. "You are sometimes a wreck. That's fine. You're something. Fault is an over-simplistic notion designed by pyrsi with overly functioning minds. Hurt?

Sometimes. Hope? We must never give up on hope no matter what. That's you included, carpenter fairy."

He started to laugh. "I'm not myself, I suppose." He quieted. "I don't remember the last time I've been myself."

"That's not true," Rock continued, her voice intensifying. "You've been yourself this whole time. Your best self? Ok, fine. Who is? But you are beautiful and you are not befit to abandon." She sat up. "Let me ask you something."

Uchitar couldn't hide a spark of curiosity.

"Let's say we could cure you today. We could take away your addiction, your depression, your weaknesses—everything that has ever happened. We could pull them from your mind and sit you here, a new ma'pyr. Who would you be?"

The moment was only slightly less weighty under the rhythm of the snoring newts. But, no, Dime was deflecting too. With her own news pounding in her mind, she tried to answer the question for herself—and found the answer startling.

"I'm waiting." Rock offered no apologies but leaned forward, a sliver of the streaming light glancing brightly against the side of her shirt. Dime hadn't really given her clothes a look; she'd changed into more of an athletic look. Tailored. Lined. She must have picked it up with her other things. Her temporary tattoos hadn't been applied in a while, and in the harsh glare of the light, she almost didn't have any. Like a fairy. Though, not. Not without hair. She supposed this was just Rock. And she'd asked a question: What would a pyr be without xyr challenges?

Uchitar shifted in place. "I don't know. I want to imagine myself as that pyr, but I can't . . . see it."

"I know," Rock said, her smile almost gloating. "And that's not because you can't see some better you. It's because without those flaws—without those struggles—you wouldn't be *you*. You'd be someone else that I've never met. You can't imagine it and I can't either.

"So," she quickly continued, "I'm not saying to stay as you are.

You need help and we'll make sure to be there for you. Your road has been challenging and it will be for a while, I fear. But I don't want you to ever lose touch with that pyr in there—our Uchitar is exactly who we all need him to be. Just have some stuff to work. That's how it goes."

Dime had been watching Luja also. Ve had extensive health training, but stayed back in the shadow, letting Rock go on. She wondered what ve thought of all this.

Rock suddenly burst out into laughter. "I'm sorry. I'm not laughing at any of it, and I don't mean to be flippant. But even if you have your own troubles to manage, will you forgive me if that image of you giving the Seats' High Guards the Soldown will keep my own spirits high for cycles to come."

She worried how Uchitar would take that, but he seemed to loosen, his wings opening behind him. Finally, he started laughing too.

"Ok. I can imagine what that means, and I think we call ours the Shaback. I'll try and trust you."

"But?" Rock tilted her head.

"I don't want to hurt Volana any more than I have, and I don't see a path forward on my own."

"You're not on your own." Rock finally leaned back. "I've never taken tzetz, but in my own ways I've felt as you have. That there wasn't a road. It's not true, the stories we tell ourselves. There's always a road. Maybe a tough one, but it's there.

"There was a time I didn't know what to do. I stayed a while in the plains and when I got back to Lodon everything had . . . collapsed. My family had moved surwes and just expected me to follow. I was alone, suddenly. Dissatisfied."

"What did you do?" Uchitar said.

"For a bit, I survived. Then, I valued myself. Then, I found new pyrsi. I decided what I could do. I found purpose." She seemed to be hesitating.

Dime thought she should add something too, but she felt

awkward with Luja sitting right there. What could she say in front of ver? The truth, she supposed. Enough of it.

"I've struggled also," Dime said. "All those cycles pyrsi told me I had it perfect. Sometimes, I did. I couldn't have a better father. I made it to a high-ranking position in the IC. The Circles," she clarified for Uchitar. "I found an amazing spouse." That hidden pang of missing Dayn again pricked her. "The two best children in Ada-ji found me." She looked warmly at Luja. "I had a lovely home, a nice fireplace—a bath! I had things I didn't even appreciate. Like being friends with the bravest resistance leader. Like having known the most brilliant agent to ever walk these lands." She waved a hand to Rock but kept her attention on Uchitar.

"I had everything I could ever want. So why did I have any right to feel lost? Why did I have any right to admit pain? When others had worse?"

She knew the answer. They all did. This was standard mental health training for young ch'pyrsi. That wasn't her point. Her point was twofold. Mostly, to say that when a pyr was falling, the lies took over. The lies filled one's mind. And it was important to talk about that. And second, to let Uchitar know, that even though he couldn't stand by his actions, his experience was not unique. He was not isolated. Volana did not help him for pity, nor would Dime. They loved him. They loved each other. They loved *all* of each pyr, the challenges too.

Together, they were a community. The sad fairy. The brooding agents. The strong Aoch. The snoring newts. And love to anyone who didn't see it that way. More love. More love, so they could grow. So they could be part of this community too.

Only love could save them from the depths.

She thought of Ador. What would he do, if he knew she'd gone poetic? Without meaning to, she smiled. Uchitar thought it was for him, she supposed, and he smiled back.

"I know I'm the young one here," Luja said, "but all I see is the three most interesting, talented, passionate pyrsi I could know."

"Lu, that's sweet," Dime murmured.

"I'm not saying it to be sweet. I'm saying I had a lot of time to think in those caves. We all did. And we've all been concentrating on how to mend the rifts that divide us, when maybe we should have—"

Both newts snapped upward, their eyes so wide that Dime could see the white around the lavender. Everyone turned to watch, likely thinking the same thing. That was too sudden. What was it? Nervous to rest a hand on them and potentially startle her large friends—after all, she wasn't even sure they were fully awake—she glanced to Luja.

Luja didn't so much speak as hum in a low, soothing tone. Stern Eyes made a gesture.

"They hear fairies," Luja mouthed. Then ve motioned to the newts, who each curled into themselves on the ground, burying their heads so that each looked like a pile of feathers: Juni's mostly white, and Stern Eyes' a mottled mix.

Understanding, Dime got as comfortable as she could, sitting in a meditation pose that she'd often employed in the one sky alley garden she could reasonably walk to from her office in the IC. It was a rather sad garden, but there had been a red archway there that sort of intrigued her. It wasn't a Lodon-style shape, but something from far away. She'd spent many a break imagining the pyr who'd constructed it, where they'd been, and what emotion had brought them to form this arch here, on an isolated IC ledge. Many shifts, she'd visited and sat under it, watching the birds fly by and gazing at the mountains in the distance. This wasn't the point, though. What had the newts heard?

Rock was no longer leaned back. She hugged her knees, her nose pressed against them as if in her own version of the newt huddle.

Uchitar's wings pulled tight, and though Dime could see his arms shaking in an alarming fashion, he'd closed his eyes and was making no sound.

Luja's eyes darted upward. Ve must be able to hear them. Dime could not. She waited, and then a faint flapping emerged. A small group, flying low, through the trees. She was sure that there were ways that valence could be used to scan for them, but she didn't feel its use. She hoped perhaps this group was not as advanced. Maybe just pyrsi who'd heard the arrest order and rushed to search.

Or perhaps a coincidence, just fairies on their way. She doubted that. Still, she felt no valence, only the flapping of their wings.

She remembered Volana referring to casters. Had it been Volana? Someone. She wondered if the High Guards were trained that way, with the expert use of valence. Perhaps not. Perhaps the Seats were not as eager to be surrounded by power other than their own.

A branch snapped above and whipped back into place, and an object clattered down through the branches, smacking the top of the vined area. Dime held her breath. Afraid, then, to release it, to make a sound that might draw them there.

Her chest pinching, she drew in air, feeling it as loud as a tornado. The wing sounds faded again, and she could not hear them. She watched Luja's eyes, knowing when ve could not hear them either.

A small shape darted through the vines. It was a chipsquip. Dime worried, somehow xe could tell on them, but, she had to stop. This was just a little friend. Perhaps this was where xe normally took shelter. With a look to the pyrsi and newts within, xe left as quickly as xe'd arrived.

Finally, Luja communicated silently with Stern Eyes, and then her child nodded. "Whoever they were, they're gone."

"Well that scared the chips out of me," Rock said with a grunt.

Dime probably made a face.

"D, stop it. Not literally. My point is, I'm thinking we ought to go. These two—" Her eyes cut over to Juni and Stern Eyes. "It's their call, but I'm thinking it's best they get out of here for now. Maybe they can convince Leader not to act quite yet. Let her know we're working it. Promise we'll check in soon."

Dime agreed. And, while she thought it would be an easy thing to tell her friends she'd see them soon, it was not. The newts had guided them, comforted them, carried them when needed be. She scooted over into Juni's arms, and she could not calm herself as she murmured to the newt and allowed herself to be tousled a bit. "Tell her one lick is fine."

Luja laughed. "She says you don't like it. You need to control your emotions."

"Tell her no. Tell her I'm done with that."

It was Stern Eyes who cooed, as if Dime had said something important, or complimentary, or who knew.

They were quiet as they watched their friends wriggle through the vines and bound back in the direction of the Beds. While full-well knowing their skills at staying hidden and moving quickly, she couldn't help but worry.

"Think they'll be seen?" Luja asked. "You know . . . *caught*?" Ve said the last word like it was a poison.

"No," Uchitar said. "Did you see them? They're amazing. No wonder the Seats had to invoke a diamond wall to keep them out and still failed." He peered off wistfully. "I hope I can see them again."

"You will," she said. If he wanted to, he certainly could. The next words felt funny, but she was shaken. "Hey, I'm accepting hugs right now." Her voice trembled.

What she didn't expect was for all three pyrsi to close in on her at the same time, causing them all to give up and sit back, laughing.

"Later," Rock said. "We are too confined in the twigs."

Dime beamed around at them. She was suddenly eager to be out of here and back into the light.

"I do have an announcement." Dime cleared her throat. She should feel more serious, but the ability to talk to her friends had lifted her up, like valence, and she felt higher than any troubles that life could roll her way.

Rock leaned back onto her hands. "Don't get your expectations up," she said to Luja and Uchitar. "It's probably about a restaurant she wants to visit."

That could be. Dime did love to eat, and not being able to relax in the establishments of Lodon was a loss she had not taken lightly. Someday. Someday. Maybe she'd try that sandwich place. They were all watching her.

"My announcement is: I am never going in a cave again."

Rock's expression shifted only slightly.

"No, I'm serious. This has been a lot of caves, and cave stories, and cave lands, and slopes and water tunnels, and cave mines, and I have no idea where the heck all this is coming from but if it's a metaphor for darkness, then I officially relinquish the depths."

"That's it? You can just relinquish them?"

"Well, you've got to try." She smiled. "With friends like you, I certainly have a better go at it." She stretched her limbs, suddenly feeling the drama.

"I am ready to rise."

"That is excellent," Rock said. "And since we can't stand in here, I suppose we should be on our way."

"Then what?" Dime asked. Maybe they should go one step at a time, but she saw something in Rock's eyes.

"What now? We stop dorking around with harmbringers and twigs, and we get to the pyrsi who could do something about all this. We stop letting them avoid it."

"I like that," Luja said, with a huge grin to Rock.

Even Uchitar seemed to perk up a little. The effects of the tzetz were still coursing through him, though even in his last swings, Dime could already see flashes of a fall. They should get him out of here. Now.

"D. We still have to go back to party place."

Yeah, she supposed they did. Showing up at Volana's after how thrilled she'd been to kick them downfield wouldn't quite be fair. At least they could rest there, talk through their options. There would have to be plans for Uchitar, though. Dime didn't want to risk him finding access to tzetz. Still, no caves!

The floorpaths stayed mostly clear as they trudged together through Pito. Luja's ability to sense someone coming was acute, and as soon as ve said to hide, they did, waiting until whoever was there had passed.

Eventually they made it to the grove where the party home rested, high above. Only then, as Uchitar wobbled upward, did Dime risk a small amount of valence and lift the three others to meet him, each clinging to their bag. She did think fondly of Rosebench, still waiting under that waterfall patio. She made a solemn pledge not to leave it there, even if Ella's and Volana's chairs became lost to the elements.

Dime stumbled through the curtain, left without words as she saw Volana and Ador sitting at a table, sharing a pitcher of something pink in color, and deep in conversation. Tum was there, in her wheelchair that Dayn had made her back up at the den.

She looked around expectantly, waiting for Dayn to pop out from a corner, or up the ramp, and rush to greet her. With a pang, she understood that Dayn was not there.

Instead, she threw a smile onto her face and bent to greet Tum, who'd wheeled frantically over to reach for Dime's hug.

"I'm here," she said. "I'm here."

"Did you do it? Did you succeed?"

Dime felt sick, inside. She'd have to tell Tum about the . . . disease, wouldn't she? Or was that too much of a burden? What had the others said—that nothing had changed. She'd hugged Tum her whole life. Should she stop now? She stalled, her arms still extended.

"Ma-ma?"

"I found out that I used to have a disease, Tum-Tum. I don't think I have it now, but it's possible it could come back. I don't . . . I don't know."

"I want a hug, Ma-ma."

Dime leaned in, embracing her child and not knowing whose tears streamed down her face.

She turned to see Volana and Uchitar in an embrace also, Uchitar muttering over and over and Volana speaking softly and calmly. Ador had stepped away.

Luja joined the two fairies, and as ve spoke, Volana rested a hand on vis arm. Only then did she notice Agni, leaping up for Dime's attention. Should she tell the kita too? Harm, why was everything complicated now?

When could she go back to her life?

What was that now?

She reached down and rubbed against the kita's ear, only mutely acknowledging the soft rumble against her fingers.

"My mothers wore out quickly," Volana explained. Maybe to Dime, but she was so distracted. "They have not been around a ch'pyr for a while; even though I tried to explain that she is not so young and perhaps the best behaved I've ever seen."

"It's odd how you forget," someone was saying. Dime stared off at the wall.

Now Rock was talking to Tum. Luja was with them. Ador moved closer, his eyes filled with concern.

"Let's get you some water and food," he said. "It seems you've all been through a lot. Do you need to rest?"

"I'm fine," she murmured. "We need to get moving. Things are bad."

"I feared as much. Volana told me what she knows, but I surmise there's more."

"There's more," she said.

"We'll get to it when you're ready." Ador helped her into a chair and was pouring some of the pink liquid into a cup. "In the meantime, I'm sorry to push. But I have some news. When you're ready."

"Might as well be now," Dime said. She tried to smile.

END OF PART 09

About the Author

E.D.E. Bell (she/e) was born in the year of the fire dragon during a Cleveland blizzard. After a youth in the mitten, an MSE in Electrical Engineering from the University of Michigan, three wonderful children, and nearly two decades in Northern Virginia and Southwest Ohio developing technical intelligence strategy, she now applies her magic to the creation of genre-bending fantasy fiction in Ferndale, Michigan, where she is proud to be part of the Detroit arts community. A passionate vegan and enthusiastic denier of gender rules, she feels strongly about issues related to human equality and animal compassion. She revels in garlic. She loves cats and trees. You can follow her adventures at edebell.com.

Conclude Dime's story in . . .

Part 10: Rise

edebell.com/diamondsong